THEY CALL ME THE NIGHT HOWLER!

GOOSEBUMPS®

Also available as ebooks

ALSO AVAILABLE:

IT CAME FROM OHIO!: MY LIFE AS A WRITER by R.L. Stine

THEY CALL ME THE NIGHT HOWLER!

R.L. STINE

SCHOLASTIC INC.

Goosebumps book series created by Parachute Press, Inc.
Copyright © 2020 by Scholastic Inc.

ISBN 978-1-338-35575-8

10 9 8 7 6 5 4 3 2 1   20 21 22 23 24

Printed in the U.S.A.   40
First printing 2020

SLAPPY HERE, EVERYONE.

Welcome to My World.

Yes, it's *SlappyWorld*—you're only *screaming* in it! Hahaha!

Want to know how old I am? What difference does it make when I'm this good-looking?! Hahaha.

I just celebrated my birthday—by throwing a cake into someone's face! Hahaha.

Sorry I forgot to blow out the candles first!

Guess that was a mistake. Someone asked me what my biggest mistake was. I think my biggest mistake is being too nice. Haha. Or is it being too generous?

Listen, we all make mistakes. I do, too. After all, I'm only inhuman! Hahaha.

I'm having a nice day. I'm sitting at home reading a book. Know what kind of book I like? A horror story where the dummy wins! Now, here's a story for you. It's about a boy named Mason who is going to face one of the nastiest and

1

weirdest supervillains ever. Think Mason will win? I don't! Hahaha.

The story is called *They Call Me the Night Howler.* And I think it's a howl!

It's just one more terrifying tale from *SlappyWorld.*

How I Became a Superhero
By Mason Brady

I'm Mason Brady, and that's the title of the paper I'd like to write for Mrs. Stuckhouse, my sixth-grade teacher.

It's an exciting story, with lots of adventure and surprises. And, trust me, all kinds of danger. And I'm sure I would get an A-plus or at least an A on it.

But, of course, I can't write it. Because it's the truth.

It has to remain a big, fat superhero secret.

If I tell anyone, I will lose all my powers. And then where would I be? Doomed. And my enemies would celebrate.

My secret identity has to remain hush-hush. Actually, I'm not even sure about it myself. I mean, it's very confusing. How many twelve-year-olds have to worry about a secret identity?

Okay. Let's put it this way—I'm trying to figure out how to tell you about who I was and who I am now and what happened in between.

Well, start at the beginning, Mason.

That's how I talk to myself sometimes. It helps me untangle my thoughts.

So here goes . . .

The story starts at my favorite place on earth. The Comic Book Characters Hall of Fame Museum.

The museum is actually an old mansion located at the edge of Fargo Hills, about an hour's drive from my house. It's high on a hill, surrounded by tall, bending trees that cast the entire building in dark shadow.

It has a round stone tower on one end and several chimneys sticking up on its slanting roof. I think it looks more like a castle than a house.

As Dad pulled the car into the parking lot, my heart was pounding. It was like a drumbeat. I could hear it bumping in my ears. That's how excited I was.

My ten-year-old sister, Stella, sat next to me in the back seat. She was pretending to be excited, too. She likes to make me nuts by copying me all the time. Stella isn't into comic books or superheroes one bit. She doesn't even know who the Avengers are. I asked her to name them and she just giggled.

Even her *looks* copy me. We're both tall. We

both have short black hair and dark eyes and serious faces.

Why does she have to look like me? It's so annoying.

For the whole drive, she kept poking me and asking dumb questions.

"Mason, would you rather have the power to fly or be invisible?"

I pushed her away. "I don't want to play that game, Stella."

She grinned at me. "If you were a superhero, what color costume would you wear?"

I knew she was only asking the questions to drive me crazy. She didn't even wait to hear my answers. "What would your superhero name be, Mason? Would you rather be good or evil? What special power would you have?"

"The power to make you shut up?" I replied.

"Stop that, Mason!" Mom snapped. She twisted around in the passenger seat. "Stella is trying to have a conversation with you."

"No, she isn't," I said. "She's just being a pest. She isn't into comics at all."

"Well, you can teach her," Dad said.

He always takes Stella's side. She's his little princess.

"You can be her tour guide," Mom said.

I groaned.

What can you say after a horrible idea like that?

I'm very serious about superheroes and comic book art. I draw my own comic strips, and I think I'm getting better and better.

My superhero is called Double-Header. That's because he has two heads. One head is good. The other head is evil. I think Double-Header is the first two-headed superhero in history.

I show my comic drawings to my friends at school. They all say I'm a genius. I can't tell if they're being sarcastic or not.

Sarcastic was one of our vocabulary words, and it's a good one. I use it a lot.

I showed one of my comics to Mrs. Stuckhouse, and she said, "Wonderful, wonderful." But she was in a hurry and hardly looked at it.

I gazed out the window as we pulled into the museum parking lot. "Wow!" I couldn't help but let out a cry when I spotted the tall bronze statue at the entrance. The statue of the Silver Centipede.

The Silver Centipede was the first superhero inducted into the Hall of Fame. And the Man of 100 Legs, as he is known, became the symbol of the museum.

One of my most awesome T-shirts has the big silvery Centipede on the front. I don't wear it very often. It's too valuable. I've tried drawing the Silver Centipede. But it's very hard. I always mess up the legs.

I leaped out of the car before Dad even shut off

the engine. "YAAAY! We're HERE!" I jumped up and down. I felt like I could explode, with my whole body flying off in different directions. That's how excited I was.

I trotted ahead of the others as we crossed the gravel parking lot toward the entrance. Dad hurried after me and put a hand on my shoulder. "Now, I know you're excited, Mason," he said. "And I want you to have the time of your life here. But I just want to ask one thing."

"Okay," I said. "What's that?"

"It's a very big museum. Don't wander off. Let's all stick together, okay?"

"Sure, Dad," I said.

I was being sarcastic.

My plan was to get away from them as fast as I could.

And, of course, that's how all the trouble started.

2

My head began to spin when we stepped into the very first room of the museum. The walls were covered with huge paintings of the greatest comic heroes of all time.

My eyes darted from painting to painting. I didn't know where to begin.

The White Raven stood next to Harvey the Horrible. Guppy Girl, with her fins of steel, was riding a tsunami across a raging ocean.

The picture of The Flattener was painted by one of my favorite comic artists, Min Li. The hero's name is really Henry Punch. But he got that nickname because he leaves his enemies as flat as pancakes.

Will I ever be able to draw this well?

That's the question I asked myself as I moved slowly across the room, studying each painting.

I wondered if Min Li or any of the other artists ever gave drawing lessons.

Stella bumped me from the side. "Where is

Captain Teddy Bear?" she asked. "I love Captain Teddy Bear."

"Go away," I said. "This is the best art ever done. Captain Teddy Bear is for little kids."

Stella made her pouty face. "I don't care. I think Captain Teddy Bear is cute." She bumped me again.

"Why don't you go to the baby room?" I said. "You can find all your favorites there. They have Goo Goo Girl and Captain Diaper Rash. That sounds like something you'd like."

"Be nice to your sister," Dad said. "She just wants to learn."

I gritted my teeth and growled.

Princess Stella can do no wrong.

I trotted away from Stella and led the way into the next room. It was filled with long glass display cases. The cases had superhero costumes inside.

I hurried to the first case and lowered my face to the glass. I couldn't believe I was gazing at Lava Lad's actual costume. It looked just like a blazing red volcano was erupting on it.

"Hey, this one is funny!" Stella exclaimed. She had her face pressed against a display case, rubbing her hands all over the glass. "It's a joke, right, Mason?"

I walked up to her. "That's not a joke," I told her. "That's The Masked Orangutan."

She squinted at me. "How can a stupid orangutan be a superhero?"

"He's not stupid," I said. "He has the wisdom of seven humans." I pushed her back. "Get your hands off the glass."

"Well, why does he wear that stupid mask?" she asked.

"It's not a stupid mask. He wears it so no one can guess his identity," I said. I let out a long sigh. I mean, how could she not know *that*?

I turned to my parents. "Stella is smearing the glass."

"Her hands are clean," Dad said. "She won't hurt anything."

Sheesh.

I had to get away from my sister. And my parents. The museum wasn't crowded. In fact, we were the only family I saw. So there was no way they'd lose me.

I waited till Stella and my parents had their backs turned, studying the blue-and-green costume of Sir Seaweed. Then I darted out of the room, through a narrow entrance at the far wall.

I found myself in a long, dimly lit hall. The walls were covered with superhero weapons. Ancient-style battle axes hung next to laser beam weapons. I hurried past silvery swords and golden bows and arrows. Flashes of lightning crackled on the ceiling over my head.

A lot of doors were closed along this hall. I didn't see anyone else back here. A wide door at the end of the hall stood partly open, pale blue light glowing behind it.

I lowered my head and took off running toward the open door. I was nearly there when I heard footsteps behind me.

I spun around.

"Oh no."

Stella came rushing at me. "Wait up! Mason, wait up!"

She ran up to me and slapped my shoulder. "Nice try, dude. But you lose. You're stuck with me." She giggled.

At least she realized she was a pain.

I just shook my head and uttered a growl. I didn't say anything.

I turned and led the way through the door. It took a little while for my eyes to adjust to the dim blue light.

When I could finally focus, I saw a tall statue in the center of the room. The hero's back faced the door. I could only see his long cape.

I took two steps toward the statue. Then I stopped when I heard a loud *slaaaam*.

I spun around. The door had banged shut behind us. I blinked to make sure I was seeing right.

And then I heard a *cliccck* as the door locked.

I turned to Stella. "Hey—what's up with that?" I murmured.

3

I ran to the door. Grabbed the knob. Pulled. It wouldn't budge.

We were locked in.

Stella and I stared at each other in silence.

We both turned to look at the statue. Two spotlights on the ceiling bathed it in an eerie blue light.

I made my way around to the front—and instantly recognized the character. I gasped. The statue captured him perfectly.

The leopard-skin cape and the white boots covered in yellow feathers gave him away. So did the crooked smile on his face and the wild, bug-eyed look in his eyes.

"This is Dr. Maniac," I told Stella.

"Well, duh," she said. She pointed to a sign on the wall. It read:

DR. MANIAC
I'M NOT CRAZY—I'M A MANIAC!

"He's weird," Stella said, squinting at the feathery boots.

"Definitely," I replied. "He's one of the weirdest characters ever."

"Is he good or bad?"

"Bad," I said. "I mean seriously bad. Dr. Maniac is one of the worst supervillains of all time. And no one can ever catch him because he's so totally twisted and unpredictable."

"I'M NOT THAT BAD!" a deep voice boomed.

I uttered a startled cry and nearly jumped out of my shoes. "Wh-who said that?" I stammered. My voice came out in a tiny squeak.

Stella grabbed my arm.

A tall man stepped from the shadows. He swept his leopard-skin cape around him. He wore steel body armor over his blue-and-green jumpsuit.

Dr. Maniac!

He glared angrily at Stella and me. "I don't like to be bad-mouthed," he said. "I don't like people saying nasty things about me. It hurts my feelings. It makes me angrier than a tadpole in a barrel of cheese curd!"

I swallowed. "I—I—I—"

I wanted to say *I'm sorry*, but I couldn't get the words out.

He was really *real*! Dr. Maniac was *real*. Superheroes were *real*!

Stella took a step forward. "My brother was just explaining to me who you are," she said.

"Who I *are*?" Maniac boomed angrily. "Who I *are*?! I'll *tell* you who I *are*! I'm the bratwurst in a bowl of baked beans! Does that give you an idea of who I *are*?"

"Not really," Stella muttered.

"I-I've read your graphic novels," I said. I was struggling to say something nice to calm him down. "You ... uh ... have a lot of personality."

"I *eat* personality for breakfast," he said. "Stick out your tongue, fella."

I gasped. "Huh? My tongue? Why?"

He took two steps toward me. His body armor rattled as he walked. "I'm a doctor, aren't I? Stick out your tongue."

I hesitated.

What would he do if I *didn't* stick my tongue out?

"Okay." I stuck out my tongue.

"Haha! Made you do it!" He pumped his gloved fists in the air as he laughed.

"Can we go now?" Stella asked in a tiny voice.

Maniac turned to her, his eyes nearly bulging from his head. One blue eye and one brown eye. "Go?" he boomed. "*Go? Before we've even had our *tea*?"

"Uh ... Stella and I don't like tea," I said.

"Neither do I!" Maniac cried.

"So can we go?" Stella asked. Her chin was

14

trembling. I could see she was as afraid as I was.

"Go?" Maniac repeated. "Don't make me *larf*! Don't make me LARF!"

"Our parents are waiting—" I started.

"How can you leave?" the supervillain demanded. "The door is locked."

"Can you unlock it?" I asked.

"Don't make me LARF! Don't make me LARF!" he shouted again, tossing his cape behind him.

"No. Really," I said. My throat suddenly felt tight. My heart was pounding. "It . . . it was nice meeting you. I've always dreamed about meeting a comic book character in person. Sometimes I even daydream that *I* am a superhero. But . . . well . . . Stella and I have to go."

Dr. Maniac rubbed his chin with one gloved hand. "Hmmmm," he murmured. "Actually, there's only one way for you to leave."

"What's that?" I asked.

"If you want to leave this room," Maniac said, "you have to eat my boot!"

I gasped. "Huh?"

Maniac reached down and tugged off one of his boots. He shoved it toward me. "Eat my boot and you're free to go."

I stared at the boot covered in long yellow feathers. "You're joking, right?" I said.

"Joking? I'm as serious as a robin redbreast eating a Tootsie Roll!" he exclaimed.

"You're crazy!" Stella cried.

"I'm not crazy! I'm a MANIAC!"

Stella took a few steps back from him. I gazed around the room, searching for a way to escape. Another door . . . a window . . . *anything*.

But except for the one locked door . . . just solid walls.

Dr. Maniac leaned against the big statue of himself. He pushed the boot against my chest. "Go ahead. Eat it. Eat my boot."

My stomach did a flip-flop. I suddenly felt sick. "I . . . I can't," I stammered.

"Go ahead," he insisted, still pushing the boot against my chest. "Eat it. It's soft. It's very soft leather. It'll go down easy. You'll see, Herman." He squinted at me. "Is your name Herman?"

"No, it's Mason."

He paused. "Are you sure?"

"Yes. It's Mason."

He nodded. "Okay. I thought maybe you were a Herman. I just took a guess. Sometimes I get it right."

He pushed the boot harder against me. "Listen, Herman, do you know how I know your name? Because I'm brilliant. Ask anyone. I'm as smart as a cow in a pizza parlor."

My stomach churned again. I had to force my breakfast back down.

I took the boot into my hands. It was heavier than I thought. The feathers were long and scratchy.

"Do I . . . do I really have to eat this boot?" I stammered.

Maniac shook his head. He took the boot from me. "No. You don't. I was just messing with you."

"Huh?" I uttered another surprised gasp.

"Just messing with you," he repeated. He slid the boot back onto his foot.

"I'm not really Dr. Maniac," he said. He pulled off his gloves and set them down on the base of the statue. "I'm an actor. I work for the museum."

"But—but—" I stammered.

17

"I was just doing my job, Mason. Playing the part of Dr. Maniac," he said. "It's all improv. I make it up as I go."

"You're very good at it," Stella said. "You had us believing."

He grinned. "Did I give you a good scare?"

We both nodded.

"Here, guys. You were good sports. Let me give you this," he said. He pulled two cards from under his armor and handed them to us. "It's a ten percent discount at the gift shop."

He pushed a button and the door slid open. Stella and I waved good-bye and strode quickly into the hall. Even though I knew the guy was just an actor, I was still eager to get out of there.

"I've got to tell Mom and Dad what happened to us!" Stella cried. She took off running down the long hall. I watched her till she disappeared around a corner.

I glanced around. "Finally," I murmured, still a little shaky from that strange guy. "Now maybe I can have some fun."

5

The next room was filled with movie posters. The movies were all based on comic book characters. As I made my way from poster to poster, I couldn't believe how many of the films I had seen.

There were a few other museum visitors in the room. A teenage couple who held hands as they admired the posters. And a family with three kids who didn't seem interested at all. They kept asking if the museum had ice cream.

I stopped in front of a poster for the movie *Don't Call Me Arthropod.*

That was one of the weirdest films I'd ever seen. It was about a family in Maine who were all slowly turning into lobsters. I thought it was funny, but I don't think it was meant to be.

The art on the poster was awesome. The artist showed the horror on the faces of the five family members as they held up their lobster claws. I studied the art for a long time. Then I took out my phone and took a photo of the poster.

My plan was to try to copy it at home.

I took a photo of the next movie poster, too. It showed an action scene with The Scolders. That's a hugely popular team of superheroes who scold criminals until they realize they are doing wrong and surrender.

Seeing all this awesome art made me want to go home and work on my drawings. Dad said I could take an art course at the city center next summer. But that's a long time to wait.

I knew I could draw this stuff. I just needed to practice and practice.

I moved to the next room. All four walls were covered in comic book covers. *I never want to leave this place!* I told myself. *It's heaven!* And it was even better seeing it *all by myself* without Stella or my parents in my face.

I studied the comic book covers for a long time. I took some photos to study them some more when I got home. Then I walked through a narrow hallway into the next room.

This room didn't look like it belonged in the museum. It looked like someone's living room, with a couch and two armchairs, and a long desk beside a dark fireplace.

I turned and started to leave. But I stopped when I spotted a man at the side of the couch. He wore a black-and-navy-blue superhero costume.

I watched him pull off the dark cape and drape

it over the back of the couch. He slid off his tall black boots.

It took me a while, but I recognized him. The Night Howler. One of my favorite superheroes.

Why was he undressing in here?

I decided I should leave and give him some privacy. But as I turned to the door, I sneezed.

WAAAACHOOO!

I don't know how to sneeze quietly.

He and I both jumped.

"S-sorry," I stammered.

He shrugged his huge shoulders. "That's okay, kid. No harm done."

His blue mask hung over the couch arm. He folded it and placed it on top of the cape. Then he raised his dark eyes to me. "Are you lost?" he asked.

"N-no," I stammered. "I'm just . . . exploring."

He nodded. Then he started to pull off his costume top.

"Are you an actor?" I blurted out. "Do you work here?"

He dropped his hands away from his costume. "Actor?"

"My sister and I," I said. "We met one of the other actors. He played Dr. Maniac."

The man's face reddened. He scowled. "Don't mention Dr. Maniac to me," he said through gritted teeth.

I swallowed. I just stood there. I didn't know what to say next.

"I'm not an actor," he said finally. "I'm the real Night Howler."

My hands suddenly felt ice-cold. My heart was fluttering in my chest. "You're real? Seriously real? I . . . I never met a real superhero," I stammered.

"Well, you have now," he replied. "Congrats, kid." He said it sarcastically.

I mean, he sounded kind of bitter. Definitely unhappy.

"I'm really into superheroes," I said. *Awkward.* But I was totally nervous. Can you blame me?

"Good for you."

He pulled his costume top over his head. He had a black T-shirt underneath.

"Are you changing into your other identity?" I asked.

"No. I'm quitting," he mumbled. He tossed the shirt onto the couch.

I gasped. "Excuse me?"

"I'm calling it quits, kid. I'm donating my costume to the museum."

"I . . . don't understand," I said. "You can't quit. You're one of the most popular superheroes in the world."

"You think being a superhero is so great?" he demanded. "How would you like to only work

22

the night shift? Never a night off. Think those are great hours?"

He didn't give me a chance to answer.

"And who do I spend all my time with? The worst bad guys on earth. Do I have any friends? No. Do I have any time for friends? No. And what would I talk about if I *did* have friends? The bad guys I'd defeated?"

"But . . . you get to be a *hero*!" I blurted out.

He frowned at me. "What do *you* know about it, kid? Do you know *anything* about me?"

"Well . . ." My mind was spinning. "I know you travel in the dark of night so that you're nearly invisible. And I know you can cast shadows over people that trap them inside. And I know you always let out a howl of attack when you go after an enemy."

He muttered something under his breath.

"And I know you've defeated a lot of super-villains," I said.

His eyes flashed. "A lot!" he repeated. "Did you know I defeated The Amazing Water-Bug? I drowned him in his own water. And I captured Gazelle Boy, the fastest villain on earth.

"And then there was Captain Mud Pie, also known as The World's Dirtiest Fighter. And The Shiver. Remember him? He always made his victims cold as ice before he robbed them. Know how I defeated him? Easy. I melted his head off!"

I couldn't believe all those supervillains were really real. "You've done a lot of good things," I said. "You made everyone a lot safer. So why do you want to quit?"

"Because I have one major failure," he said, lowering his eyes. "One villain I have tried to capture my entire career. One evil character I dream about . . . have nightmares about. And no matter how many times I try, he always gets away."

He bent and started to pull off his long black socks. "That's why I'm giving it up. Tossing in the towel. Because I'm a failure. I couldn't defeat the foe I was desperate to put away."

He tossed the socks on top of the rest of the costume. He stood there shaking his head.

I gathered my courage. "Who is it?" I managed to choke out. "Who is the supervillain?"

He gritted his teeth. "Dr. Maniac," he said in a harsh whisper.

I gasped. "I told you. My sister and I just ran into him here in the museum."

He shook his head. "That was Carlos, the actor who plays him. He does a pretty good job. But trust me, kid, he doesn't capture the pure insane evil of the real Dr. Maniac."

"Well . . . that's why you can't give up," I said. "How can you quit when you know his evil is still out in the world?"

"Easy," he said.

"But ... but ..." I sputtered. "You're a great hero. You can catch Dr. Maniac. You have to keep trying."

He hesitated for a moment. Then he gathered up his costume—and shoved it into my arms.

"You think it's so important? You think it's so exciting? So much fun? YOU try it. Congrats, kid. You're the new Night Howler."

"No, wait!" I cried.

I tried to shove the costume back to him, but he ducked away.

"I can't do it!" I shouted. "I'm just a kid. I'm twelve years old!"

"So what?" he snapped back. "You have the desire. I can see it in your eyes."

"No. No way," I pleaded.

He began circling the room, watching me. I hurried after him, trying to return the costume.

"I can't be the Night Howler! I have homework!" I shouted.

We both broke up laughing at the same time. We both realized how ridiculous that sounded.

"Stop backing away," I said. "Listen to me. Seriously, how can I be the Night Howler? Sure, I'm into superheroes. But I'm a normal kid. I don't have any powers."

"The powers are all in the costume," he replied. "Look at me. What's your name, kid?"

"Mason Brady," I said.

"Mason, my name is Cory. I don't have any powers, either. The powers of the Night Howler are all inside the costume."

"You mean—"

"When you put on the costume, you're a super-hero. You can hide in the night shadows. You can throw shadows over people and capture them. All that good stuff."

"And when you take off the costume—?"

"You're *you* again," Cory answered. "No powers. No nothing. Just your normal self."

I gazed down at the costume balled up in my hands. And felt a surge of excitement rise up over my body.

The blue-and-black cape and tights felt heavy, as if they were made for winter. It was serious clothing, not lightweight. And way too big for me. The boots were way bigger than my feet!

"I can't wear it," I said. "It's *your* size, not mine."

"When you put it on, it will fit perfectly," Cory said. "I told you, the costume is magic."

I gazed at it. I had this funny thought: *Where will I hide it in my room?*

Yes. I was actually thinking of taking it.

Something in the back of my brain was saying: *Mason, you can do this. Mason, this is something you've always dreamed of. A superhero. Maybe you were BORN to be a superhero.*

Insane thoughts. Of course, I should have

27

tossed the whole thing to the floor and run out of there as fast as I could.

But something held me back. A force that became stronger and stronger as I stared at the cape and tights and mask.

"Well . . . maybe . . ." I started.

Cory's eyes locked on mine. He took a few steps toward me. "You're seriously thinking of doing it, aren't you?" he said.

"Uh . . . yes," I murmured.

Cory rubbed his chin. "Well . . . there's one major catch," he said.

7

The costume fell from my arms and hit the floor. It spread out in front of me, as if it were alive. "Catch?" I said.

Cory nodded. "Yes. It's an important one. You see, you can't let anyone know that you, Mason Brady, are the Night Howler. Aside from me. Only former Night Howlers can know the secret."

"You mean—"

"No one can know. Not your parents. Not anyone else in your family. Not your friends. If you have a dog or a cat, don't even tell it to them."

My brain started to spin again. "What happens if someone finds out my secret identity?" I asked.

"Mason, if someone finds out that you are the Night Howler, the costume will lose all its powers. It will be just like any ordinary Halloween costume. You will be helpless."

"But now I know you're the Night Howler. Does that mean you don't have powers anymore?"

"Inviting a new Night Howler doesn't count. If

you don't accept, I'll just fog your memory. You'll forget this ever happened."

I bent and started to gather the costume up off the floor. "I know I can keep the secret," I said. "My only problem is my sister, Stella. She's a serious snoop. She's always in my room, snooping around."

"Think you can find a place to hide the costume from Stella?" he asked. He scooped up the mask and handed it to me.

Under my bed?

In my underwear drawer?

Behind the sled at the back of my closet?

"I'll think of something," I said.

"Then you're going to do it? You're going to take over as the Night Howler?"

I nodded.

Why did I suddenly feel sick to my stomach?

"Wait. One thing," I said. "How will I know when I'm needed? How will I learn about my missions?"

"You have a phone, right?" Cory said.

I nodded.

"Well, listen for a long, low buzz. That's the signal. Check your phone and a text will tell you where to go."

"But . . . who is sending the text message?" I asked.

He shrugged. "Beats me. It's a secret. Nobody knows."

Cory handed me a large museum shopping bag. "Tuck the costume in here," he said. "Tell your family it's gifts you bought at the gift shop."

He helped me shove the long cape into the bag.

"Now here's what we'll do," he said. "I'll come by your house tonight and take you out for your first try. You know. Show you the superhero ropes."

"Awesome," I said.

Tonight? So soon?

Cory walked me to the door. He was still in his black T-shirt. "One thing you should do, Mason," he said.

"What's that?"

"Practice your howl. It's very important. It's your trademark, remember."

A short while later, I was walking down the hall, searching for my family.

Did that really happen? I asked myself.

Of course it happened. I had the shopping bag in my hand.

I made a stop in the souvenir shop, then I found Mom and Dad at the entrance to the movie poster room. They came hurrying up to greet me. "I thought we were going to stick together," Dad said.

"Sorry," I said. "I didn't mean to wander away. But then I lost track of time. I just kept moving from room to room. It was awesome." I was *dying* to tell them the truth. But, of course, I couldn't.

"What's in the shopping bag?" Mom demanded.

"This superhero actor gave me ten percent off. So I bought some gifts for my friends," I said.

"Did you enjoy the museum?" Dad asked. "Was it everything you thought it would be?"

I didn't get a chance to answer.

Mom suddenly let out a cry. "Hey—where's Stella?" She glanced around.

We all spun in a circle, our eyes searching the long halls.

"She was right here," Mom said. "Where is she? Where did she go?"

SLAPPY HERE, EVERYONE . . .

Haha. Maybe Mason should slip on the Night Howler costume and go search for Stella in the shadows. This could be his first adventure as a superhero.

Or . . . perhaps as a super*ZERO*!

Mason may think he's brave enough to go out prowling at night. But my guess is, he'll be hiding under the covers when Cory comes to call. Hahaha!

I'M the one with amazing powers! Don't believe me?

I have the power to make you turn the page! Watch . . .

"I told Stella to stay close by," Dad said, peering down the long empty hall. He turned to me. "This is *your* fault, Mason. If you hadn't wandered off without her . . ."

Everything has to be my fault.

"She's probably in the Captain Teddy Bear room," I said. "Stella goes gaga for that stupid bear."

"Don't try to be funny," Dad said. "Your sister has disappeared."

"Maybe we should split up and search," I said. "One of us will find her."

"Then we'll *never* find each other," Mom said. Her chin was quivering. That always happens when she's really tense or upset.

"Why don't you two wait here?" I said. "I'll run down the hall. I'm sure I'll find her. Wait here, and I'll bring her right back."

Mom and Dad exchanged worried glances. "Okay," Dad said finally. "We'll have a seat on that bench and wait for you. But find her fast, Mason."

I left my shopping bag with them and trotted down the long hall. Mom and Dad had no business getting so terrified instantly. But . . . that's just how they are. They're always in a panic.

If they had any idea that I was about to become the Night Howler and go out after villains at night, they'd lock me in my room forever, and that's how I'd spend the rest of my life.

I peeked into the room with the Captain Teddy Bear costume display. I had been wrong. No sign of Stella. The next room was also for little kids. It was filled with posters and comic art of Raptor Junior.

No sign of Stella in there, either.

I turned the corner and stepped into the next hall. And that's when I heard a scream. Stella's scream.

And a second later, she came into view. Screaming her head off. In horrible trouble.

"HEY—!"

My shout rang off the stone walls.

Stella shrieked and flung both arms in the air as a tall, ugly creature carried her across the hall.

Whoa. It was half man, half garden slug, and Stella seemed stuck to its back.

She bumped up and down, her hair flying, as it ran full speed, its pale boots thudding the floor.

"Help! Helllllp!" Stella's cries froze me in place.

I finally recognized the creature. It was The Living Larva.

One of the meanest, ugliest, ickiest super-villains in all of comics.

"Stop!"

I tried to scream. But my voice came out in a raspy whisper.

They had disappeared from view. But I could still hear the Larva's thudding footsteps and my sister's shrill yelps of horror.

I took a deep breath and ran after them.

"Put her down! Put my sister down!" I finally found my voice and shouted as I chased them.

I saw them vanish into the Villains Veranda. The museum map said it was an outdoor terrace where the supervillains gathered.

Ducking my head, forcing my aching legs to go faster, I burst after them into the veranda.

I saw Stella standing on the floor. She was straightening her hair with both hands and laughing. The Living Larva stood across from her. He was laughing, too.

My heart pounding, I rocketed up to them. "Stella—what—?" I choked out.

They both turned, surprised to see me. "Hey, Mason," Stella said calmly, still grinning. "So cool. The Living Larva is giving piggyback rides in the Kids' Lounge."

She raised her gaze to him. "That was awesome! Thanks!"

He gave her a gooey, two-fingered salute. "Stay evil, kid," he said. That's his big slogan. "I gotta go. I got a long line of Larva lovers back in the lounge."

He spun away and jogged to the veranda door.

I frowned at Stella. "Mom and Dad started to panic. You disappeared."

"*You* disappeared first!" she snapped back. "I got tired of waiting for you."

I led the way back to the main hall. "That Larva dude is nice," Stella said. "He's kind of sticky. But nice."

"He's just an actor," I told her. "The *real* Living Larva is not nice. Believe me, he doesn't give piggybacks."

"You think you know everything," she muttered.

"What's *that* supposed to mean?" I said.

She didn't have time to answer. Mom and Dad came rushing forward and showered her with hugs.

"Where were you?"

"Why did you run off?"

"We were so worried."

I waited patiently until the whole emotional scene was over. "Is it time to go?" I asked Dad.

He checked his watch. "Yes. We'll be in some traffic, but we have to start for home."

Traffic is one of Dad's least favorite things. He talks about traffic all the time.

I took my shopping bag from Mom and headed toward the front entrance. "Hey—!" I cried out as Stella grabbed the bag from my hands.

"What's in this?" she demanded.

I grabbed it back. "None of your business."

Mom tapped my shoulder. "Be nice to your sister, Mason. She asked you a simple question."

"Just some gifts," I muttered. "Souvenir things for my friends."

"Seriously?" Stella said. She grabbed the bag again and swung it out of my reach.

And before I could stop her, she pulled it open—and began pawing through the stuff inside.

10

"What *is* this junk?" she cried.

She lifted out a Captain Salamander action figure. Then a bandanna just like the one The Amazing Ms. Tortoise wears.

"I told you," I said. "Just souvenirs. From the gift shop." I grabbed the bag back. "Get your paws off my stuff."

"Mason, don't be rude," Mom scolded.

I straightened the souvenirs in the bag. I know my sister too well. I knew exactly what she would do when she saw the shopping bag. She'd grab it from me and begin pulling the stuff out and demanding to know what it was.

If she saw the costume . . . if she figured out I was now the Night Howler . . . the costume would lose all its powers before I even had a chance to try it on.

So I had carefully rolled up the costume and tucked it into my backpack before I went to the

40

gift shop. Then I used the bag for some souvenirs I bought.

The Night Howler costume was safe and sound, at least for now. My first important job was to find a place to hide it where my sister couldn't find it and destroy its powers.

I thought about this problem all the way home.

I knew my closet wasn't safe from Stella. And she was always digging through my dresser drawers. She wasn't looking for anything in particular. She was just being nosy.

Believe me, I knew what Stella would be when she grew up. She'd be a *spy*.

Anyway, as we drove toward home, Stella seemed very excited about the museum. She kept jabbering away. I didn't really listen. I was concentrating on thinking up a safe hiding place.

But I suddenly paid attention when I heard her say this:

"I'm going to start drawing my own comic strip. Just like Mason, only mine will be better."

Stella is such a total copycat.

"Who is your superhero going to be?" I asked.

"The Living Larva," she answered. "Only, in my comics he'll be nice."

I groaned. That was the worst idea I'd ever heard.

"And what will his power be?" I demanded.

"Giving piggyback rides," she said.

I groaned again.

"Mason, stop making fun of your sister," Mom said, turning around in the passenger seat. "You should encourage her."

"Why?" I said.

"Don't be a smart guy," Dad snapped. "I'm sure Stella has a lot of art talent."

"For sure," I murmured.

Stella gave me a hard shove in the ribs, but I ignored it.

At home, I carried the shopping bag and the backpack up to my room. My head was spinning. Where was the best place to stash the costume? Everywhere I looked, I saw a place that my snoopy sister could find.

How about the basement? I asked myself.

It seemed like a good idea for a minute or two. But then I realized it wouldn't work at all. What if there was an emergency? What if I needed to change into the costume and get moving immediately?

The basement was too far away. Also, it would look totally suspicious if I kept disappearing into the basement all the time. My family would figure out very quickly that something weird was going on.

I sat on my bed, gripping the backpack in my lap. I gazed all around the room. Behind the bookshelves? Under my desk? No. No.

I jumped up and began to pace back and forth.

My bedroom is long and narrow. Perfect for pacing. I walked holding the backpack in front of me. Thinking . . . thinking.

And then a squeak beneath my shoe gave me the answer.

11

The loose floorboard.

Why hadn't I thought of that sooner?

I dropped to my knees and grabbed at the board. I dug my fingernails into the crack and pried the board up. Then I peered down into the empty space below.

Yes! There was enough room to drop it in and push it under the floorboard next to it. Stash it completely out of sight. I could keep it down there, and it would be close to me at all times.

My heart started to race with excitement. I felt so good. The problem was solved. My super-hero secret would be safe.

I turned to the bedroom door. Closed. No way Stella could see me.

I pulled the costume and mask from my back-pack. My hands trembled as I rolled everything up and shoved it into the narrow space. Then I carefully replaced the board and pressed it into place.

I walked back and forth on the board a few times, just to make sure it would stay down. Then I tossed my backpack onto my bed and carried the shopping bag with all the souvenirs into my closet.

If Stella wanted to snoop some more in the shopping bag, fine. No problem.

She could snoop in my closet all she wanted. She wouldn't find anything interesting.

Feeling a lot better, I pulled open the door to my room. I could hear Stella whistling to herself in her room across the hall. She's a much better whistler than I am. But so what?

"Dinner! Come downstairs!"

I heard Dad's shout.

I started to the stairs. I heard Stella stop whistling. "Coming!" I shouted.

I was halfway down the stairs when I saw a blur of movement out of the corner of my eye.

Was that Stella? Did she just run into my room?

No. That wasn't possible—was it?

You're just nervous, I told myself.

Shaking my head, I made my way downstairs. I had just entered the kitchen when I heard Stella's shouts from upstairs.

"Hey—look what I just found! Hey, Dad—look what I found!"

12

I made a loud gulping sound. I felt my heart leap up into my throat.

How could she have found my secret so soon?

Mom and Dad were staring at me. "Are you okay, Mason?" Mom asked. "You suddenly went pale."

"I . . . uh . . . am just excited about dinner," I stammered.

I turned and started to race toward the stairs. But Dad was already halfway up. "What did you find up there, Stella?" he called. "Where are you?"

"In Mason's room," she shouted back.

My heart leaped around again. My knees started to fold as I followed Dad. "Hey, wait—" I choked out.

But Dad was already stepping into my room.

I hurried up behind him and stopped in the doorway. Stella was down on the floor. She had the loose floorboard in her hands.

"What's that?" Dad asked.

"I found a loose floorboard in here," Stella answered. She held it up and waved it at Dad.

He scratched his head. "How did you find it?"

"What were you doing in my room?" I cried. My voice came out more shrill than I intended.

"I just came in to return your scissors," Stella said, pointing to the scissors on my desk. "And when I started to leave, the floor squeaked under my foot. And I saw that the board was loose."

And did she also see my costume jammed down there?

No. Because she would have pulled it out. She would be asking a million questions about it.

Maybe Stella wasn't such a great snoop after all. The costume was right below the floor—right under her snooping nose—and she didn't see it.

I realized I was holding my breath. I knew I wouldn't breathe again until the board was safely back in place, and my secret was safe, too.

"Put the board down," Dad told Stella. "And I'll be right back." He spun around, moved past me, and left the bedroom.

Stella sat there with the board in her hand. She turned to me. "What's your problem, Mason? Why are you staring at me like that?"

"Uh . . . I'm not staring," I said.

Please put the board down. Please . . .

And don't look into the space.

She kept her gaze on me.

"I'm just glad you found that," I said, pointing to the board in her hand. "I didn't know it was loose. I could have tripped or something and hurt myself."

Stella laughed. "Guess I saved your life. You owe me, Mason."

Just put the board down.

I let out a long breath as she lowered the board to the hole and pressed it hard.

She didn't see the costume. I'm safe!

Dad burst back into the room. He had a hammer in one hand. His other hand was closed in a tight fist.

I moved toward him quickly. "Whoa. Wait. Dad—what are you going to do?"

He didn't answer. He dropped down to the floor beside Stella. "Which board is it?" he asked her.

Stella pointed.

Dad opened his fist. He had a bunch of long nails in his hand.

"No. Wait—!" I cried again.

He looked up at me. "What's wrong? I'm just going to nail this board down so it won't be dangerous."

"Well..." My brain froze. Totally froze. I couldn't think of anything to say. I couldn't think of a single reason to convince him to take away his hammer and nails.

I watched in silent horror as he pounded four nails into the ends of the board. Stella had this

48

weird smile on her face. Maybe she really did believe that she'd saved my life.

"Now, let's go have dinner," Dad said. Stella followed him out the door. I took one last look at my floor. Then I made my way downstairs to the kitchen.

Dad spent most of dinner complaining about how the house was falling apart. "The house is only five years old, and it's a tumbledown wreck," he said.

Mom tried to calm him. "It was only one floorboard," she told him. "One floorboard doesn't mean a wreck."

He grumbled and grouched. I didn't pay any attention to most of it. Actually, I hardly heard a word Dad said. I guess I was lost in my own thoughts.

I knew that tonight was my night for adventure. Tonight wasn't an ordinary night. Tonight my life was supposed to change forever. But that would be impossible now. No way I could reach my costume.

Sure enough, at a little after nine, I was just finishing up my homework, filling in the last part of my science notebook, when I heard a sharp tapping on my bedroom window.

I spun away from my desk—and saw the Night Howler in the window.

He was in a costume. How was that possible?

His dark eyes peered through his mask into my room. His hands held on to the window frame. He swung his legs into the room and landed hard. His boots made a heavy *thud*.

"Hey—" I uttered a cry.

His cape was caught on the windowsill. He tugged it free and swept it behind him. Then he turned to me and squinted through the mask.

"You're not ready," he said.

"I know." I sighed. "There's a problem." And then I added, "I thought you gave your costume to me. But . . . you're wearing the Night Howler costume."

"I found a spare in my closet," he said. "But . . . why aren't you ready? You knew I was coming tonight."

I crossed the room to the floorboard and pointed down. "My costume. I hid it under the floor. And then my dad nailed the board down. No way I can get it."

He rubbed his chin with one gloved hand. He stared at the floor. Then he sighed. "Oh, wow. I'm so sorry. I'm truly sorry it didn't work out."

He raised his eyes to me and lowered his voice. "Now I have to destroy you."

SLAPPY HERE, EVERYONE.

Hahaha. This story turned out a *lot* shorter than I had imagined.

What a loser. I thought Mason would at least give us a few adventures before the whole thing came to an end.

Maybe he should forget the costume and just go out in his underwear.

He could change his name to Captain Underpants! Hahaha.

Or has someone already done that?

13

A terrified squeak escaped my open mouth. My breath caught in my throat. My legs started to tremble.

He put a hand on my shoulder. "Sorry, dude. That's my idea of a joke." Cory raised both gloved hands. "I admit it. I have a cruel streak. Something I've gotta work on. I'm not proud of it."

"You mean—?" I started.

"We can get the costume from under the floor," he said. "No biggie."

I let out a long whoosh of air. My heart started to beat again. "Should I go get a hammer?"

He shook his head. "No way. I want to show you some of the powers you have. Call your father. Tell him to get up here. He'll get the costume for us."

I blinked. "Huh? What do you mean?"

"Just call him," Cory said.

"But . . . he'll *see* you!" I cried.

"Call him."

So I shouted for my dad to come up. He was in the den watching some kind of reality dating show with Mom. Dad hates those shows. But Mom doesn't like to watch alone.

I heard Dad's thudding footsteps coming up the stairs. "What's the problem, Mason?" he called.

He stepped into my room and stopped. His eyes went wide when he saw the Night Howler standing beside me. "What—?"

Cory raised his right arm slowly. He gestured with his fingers.

I gasped as a dark shadow formed above our heads, like a small cloud. The shadow floated quickly, silently over my dad.

For a moment, Dad was hidden behind the dark cloud. Then the cloud lifted and he stood there, covered in a charcoal-colored shadow.

His mouth remained open in surprise. His expression didn't change. He appeared frozen at first, like a gray statue. Then he began to turn his head, gazing around, confused.

Cory said, "I used my shadow powers to cloud his mind. Quick, Mason. Tell him to go get a claw hammer and pull up the floorboard."

"Will he do it?" I asked, my voice tiny.

"Would I lie to you?" Cory replied. "Hurry. We have a dangerous criminal to capture on your first mission."

"D-dangerous?" I choked out.

"Hurry."

"Dad," I started. My voice cracked. "Go get your claw hammer and pry up that loose floorboard."

I squinted into the gray shadow. Dad was all black-and-white, as if the color had been drained from him.

"No problem," he said. He spun to the bedroom door. "I'll be right back."

I listened to him hurry down the stairs.

"Will he remember any of this?" I asked Cory.

Cory shook his head. "No. When I lift the shadow, he won't remember a thing."

"That's a totally cool power!" I exclaimed.

Cory nodded. "That's why they pay me the big bucks, kid." He patted my shoulder. "And now, as soon as you get your costume on, the power will be yours."

I swallowed. Have you ever been excited and terrified at the same time? It was a whole new feeling for me.

Well, Cory's plan worked perfectly. Dad returned to my room, still in shadow. He dropped down to the floor and pried the floorboard up with his hammer.

"Tell him to take out the costume," Cory ordered.

I told Dad to pull it up and hand it to me. Dad obeyed perfectly. A few seconds later, I held the blue-and-black Night Howler costume in my arms.

"I forgot how heavy it is," I told Cory.

He pointed at it. "That's where the magic happens," he said. He motioned to my dad. "Tell him to go back downstairs."

"Dad, thanks for helping. You can go downstairs now," I said.

We waited until Dad was at the bottom of the stairs. Then Cory waved his fingers in the air again to remove the shadow over him. "He won't remember a thing, Mason."

He gave me a push. "Hurry. Get into your costume. We're late."

I scrambled into the black tights and the dark blue satiny top. I swirled the long cape around me. It took me a while to get it right, but I finally managed to pull the mask over my head and set my eyes behind the eyeholes.

Cory looked me up and down. "Okay, dude. We have a dangerous night in store. Are you ready to capture your first real criminal?"

"No, I'm not," I said.

14

Cory frowned at me. "What's wrong?"

"It's the cape," I said. "I can't figure out how to snap it shut." I fingered the satiny cloth around my neck.

"It doesn't snap," he said. "It's Velcro." He reached for the cape with both hands and closed the top. "That makes it easier to get it on and off if you're in a tight jam."

I swept the cape back. "Are we going to be in a tight jam tonight?" I asked.

He nodded. "Probably."

I took a few steps toward my bedroom door. The costume felt heavy. I could feel a low current pulsing through my body. My arm muscles were suddenly tight. I felt stronger. My shoes thudded heavily on the floor.

I heard the TV downstairs. "My parents will see us come down," I said. "How do we get out of the house?"

"No problem," Cory said softly. He raised his

hand and wiggled his fingers. A dark cloud formed above us. It lowered itself and covered us in shadow.

I squinted, struggling to see through the dark mist. Then I followed Cory down the stairs. We walked right past my parents, and they didn't take their eyes from the TV screen.

"Wow. It's almost like being invisible," I whispered.

We were out the front door and into a warm, cloudy night. A pale half moon sat low over the houses. The air felt heavy and damp.

"Stay in the shadow cloud," Cory said, close beside me. "You can travel inside the cloud. It's almost as good as flying."

I followed him as he took off running. He was right. The shadow cloud seemed to carry us. I felt my feet lift off the ground as we crossed the street. The darkness seemed to propel me forward.

Cory and I were floating over cars, carried by the mists, moving faster than I could ever run. The powers of the amazing costume raced through my body, the powers that were now MINE.

I felt awesomely brave—until I remembered why we were out here.

Cory had his eyes straight forward, his arms down at his sides. I floated closer to talk to him. "Where are we going?"

"Manders Park," he said, without slowing down. "On the other side of town."

"Wh-why?" I stammered.

"There's someone I've been trying to capture," he replied. We whirled around a corner and kept floating. "A cheap thief who hangs out there. He waits for old people to go out for a late walk. And then he grabs them from behind and robs them."

"And . . . and I'm supposed to capture him?" I stammered. I suddenly felt weak with fear.

Cory nodded. "That's your mission, Night Howler." We turned another corner. A wide area, black against the pale moonlight, came into view at the end of the next street. Manders Park.

"Use the shadow cloud," Cory said. "And use the powers of your costume."

"But . . . what if this thief tries to hurt me?" I choked out. I wanted to sound brave. But my voice came out high and whiny.

"I picked this mission for you because it's a good first job," Cory replied. "The thief is named The Quitter. Don't quit until you have defeated him and taken him prisoner."

"But—but—" I sputtered.

We were swallowed in darkness as we floated into the park. I squinted through the trees and saw a faint yellow light. I followed the light to a path that twisted under pale streetlamps.

The park appeared empty. A strong gust of wind shook the trees and made them whisper. An old newspaper on a park bench made a rattling sound as the wind tossed its pages.

The path curved around a small supply shed. A

bronze statue of a German shepherd stood guard at the side of the shed.

I uttered a sharp cry when I heard a scream on the wind.

I stopped short. Under a streetlamp up ahead, I saw an old, white-haired couple, a man and woman in long raincoats. They had their hands raised above their heads.

They stared openmouthed at a huge man wrapped in an enormous black coat, with a black ski mask pulled down over his head. He was barking words at them, and they were quivering in fear.

The Quitter!

There he was.

My legs suddenly started to give way. I forced myself to keep standing. But panic shot through my body. My teeth began to chatter, and shudder after shudder ran down my back.

This is really happening.

I can't do this.

Why did I think I could do this?

Was I out of my mind?

"I'm sorry," I told Cory. "I'm not as brave as I thought I was. I can't—"

I spun around. "Cory? Hey—Cory?"

He had disappeared.

I was on my own.

15

I could see the terror on the couple's faces. The Quitter had his back to me. I watched him grab the man's wallet.

I had no choice.

I had to take him down.

I raised my hand and moved my fingers the way Cory had done. Yes! A dark shadow lowered over me. I was invisible. But did that mean I was safe?

I knew my only chance was to take the thief by surprise.

I could feel the powers of my costume begin to hum. A pulsing current gave me strength.

I tossed back my head. Took a deep breath. And let out the famous terrifying *howl* of the Night Howler.

"Aaaaaaaaawooooooooooooooh!"

The thief let out a startled scream. The old couple held on to each other, their faces tight with terror.

The thief dropped the wallet onto the walk and spun around to face me.

His eyes were wide behind his ski mask. Of course, he couldn't see me. I was deep in shadow.

My heart pounded like crazy. The current surged through me.

Now what?

Now what?

He raised both hands above his head. "I quit!" he cried. "You've got me. I recognized your howl, Night Howler. You win. I quit."

He picked the wallet up from the ground and handed it back to the old man. I could see that the couple was totally confused and still frightened.

"You can go home," I told them. "You're safe now."

They turned and started to walk away quickly. "Thank you, Night Howler. Wherever you are," the woman called back.

I grabbed the thief by the shoulders and pulled him inside the deep shadow.

"Don't hurt me!" he cried. "I quit. Really. I quit. They don't call me 'The Quitter' for nothing!"

I had to chuckle. Cory had picked the *best* first case for me. The Quitter had to be the wimpiest thief in history!

Riding in the shadow, I brought the Quitter to the police station two blocks from the park. I lifted the shadow. A cop hurried to greet us. His nametag read SERGEANT GARCIA.

He grabbed the Quitter. "Good work, Night Howler," he said. "How did you get this guy?"

"It was simple. He just quit," I said.

Garcia laughed. "Wish they were all this easy." His smile faded. "Hey, Night Howler, I heard you were retiring."

"Huh? *Me?*" I shook my head. "No way, Sergeant Garcia. I'm not retiring. I'm just starting."

Just for fun, I tossed back my head and let out the Night Howler howl:

"Aaaaaaaaaawooooooooooooooh!"

I hurried home. It was nearly midnight. If Mom and Dad heard me come in, I'd be in major trouble. How could I explain what I was doing out this late at night in this costume?

I had one big victory under my belt. I didn't want my superhero career to end after just one adventure.

The house was dark and silent. I tiptoed up the stairs to my room. Across the hall, Stella's door was open. Her room was dark. She had to be sound asleep.

But I didn't turn on my bedroom light till my door was tightly closed.

Safe.

I pulled off the heavy costume and tossed it onto my bed. Then I crossed the room to my dresser, pulled out a pair of pajamas, and tugged them on.

I sat down on the edge of the bed and started to fold up the costume.

That's when the bedroom door swung open and Stella came bursting in. Her pink nightshirt was twisted. Her hair stood out in tangles on the sides of her head.

She blinked a few times, then squinted at me. "Mason? You're awake?"

Before I could answer, she lowered her eyes to the costume in my lap.

Her eyes grew wide and she pointed. "Huh? What's THAT?"

16

My brain froze for a moment. Was this it? Was this the end?

I had to think fast.

"It's a Halloween costume," I said. "Grandma Pearl sent it."

"But it's spring," Stella replied. "Why would she send you something for Halloween?"

"She probably found it in some bargain store," I said, feeling beads of sweat roll down my forehead. "You know how much she likes bargains."

Stella laughed. "Did you ever go to the supermarket with her? She always picks the egg cartons that have one or two broken eggs inside. She knows the manager will sell it to her cheaper."

"The costume is way too big," I said. "Check it out." I held up the tights for Stella to see.

She laughed. "Grandma Pearl always thinks we're enormous. Remember that sundress she sent me? It was too big for Mom!"

We both laughed. My laugh was phony.

I held my breath. Did Stella really believe I was holding a Halloween costume?

She yawned. "I heard you moving around in here. Why are you trying on costumes in the middle of the night?"

"Couldn't sleep," I said. Not a great answer. But I could see she was buying it.

She yawned again. "Good night."

I followed her to the door. I waited until she was back in bed, then I closed my door again.

I wiped the sweat off my forehead with the back of my hand. "That was a close one," I muttered to myself.

I folded up the Night Howler costume, tucked it into the hole in my floor, and lowered the floorboard over it. Then I climbed into bed and hoped I could fall asleep.

I didn't have another close call until two nights later.

17

My friend George Browning and his twin brother, Walter, invited me to a sleepover at their house on Saturday night. I love hanging with these guys because they're all about fun. What's the best way to describe them? Party animals?

They're both always in trouble with Mrs. Stuckhouse in school. Not for anything serious. Just for goofing around or messing up their home-work, or for their famous laughing fits that always get the whole class giggling out of control.

One of the twins' longest laughing fits went viral on Instagram with more than three thou-sand likes. That's how funny it was. But their parents didn't think it was funny. They had to go to school and have a long discussion with our principal, Mr. Santini.

It must not have been a happy discussion. Because when their parents returned home, they took away George's and Walter's phones for a month and shut down their Instagram accounts.

I agreed with my two friends that it was unfair. I mean, laughing isn't exactly a crime, is it?

Anyway, when Dad dropped me off in the driveway to their house, I could hear loud voices from inside. And their little dog, Spartacus, was yapping his head off.

I had my sleeping bag under one arm. We were all going to sleep on the floor of their huge basement rec room. And I had packed my Night Howler costume in my backpack—just in case I was called out on a mission.

Through the front window, I saw George and a couple of other guys in the living room. They were just standing and talking.

I knocked on the front door. It swung open instantly, and I gasped. I was staring at an ugly monster, green face, two rows of enormous jagged yellow teeth, three bulging eyes, and a long forked tongue hanging limply down like a snake.

"Hi, Walter," I said.

He stood there for a moment. "How'd you know it was me, Mason?"

"The three eyes," I said. "That gave you away."

"Ha." He stepped back and let me enter the house. It was hot inside and the air smelled of pizza. I saw two large pizzas in open boxes on the living room coffee table.

Walter took my sleeping bag and backpack and tossed them down the basement stairs.

"Hey, Mason—what's up?" Alonso Ferrer called. He stood next to another guy in my class, Mickey Rowse. (Of course, we call him Mickey Mouse.) George kept punching Mickey on the shoulder for some reason.

I stepped over to them. "Why are you punching him?" I asked George.

"Because I don't have a punching bag," George answered.

It wasn't that funny, but we all laughed.

"We're all here. We can start the video," Walter said.

I spun around. "Video?"

"That's why I'm wearing this monster mask," Walter said.

"You're wearing a mask?"

More laughter.

"Pizza first," Alonso said. He grabbed a slice from one of the boxes.

"Where are your parents?" I asked George.

He motioned toward the steps. "They're hiding upstairs. They said we should have a good time. But *not* such a good time that the police have to come."

Mickey slid a pizza slice from the box. "Why are we doing a video?" he asked Walter.

Walter shrugged. "Why not?"

"I thought we were just going to hang out," I said.

"We're going to hang out in the video," Walter replied.

"Walter wants to start a new YouTube channel," George said, crushing an empty can of Coke in one hand. "He thinks it will make us rich."

I finished a slice and grabbed another.

Walter burped really loud. It echoed from behind the mask. The twins are serious burpers. I mean, their burps are *inhuman*! They did an amazing burping video on Instagram. It didn't go viral, but if burping was an Olympic sport, they'd both be wearing gold.

"Hey, Mason, how was the comic art museum?" Mickey asked. He wiped tomato sauce off his chin.

"Uh . . . pretty interesting," I said.

I thought about my Night Howler costume rolled up in my backpack. If I received the Mission Alert signal on my phone, what would I do? How would I get into my costume and get out of here without my friends noticing?

A good question.

I crossed my fingers, hoping there wouldn't be a Mission Alert tonight.

"The museum has a lot of cool stuff," I told Mickey. "It's huge. I couldn't see it all. The movie posters were awesome. And they have some of the real costumes that superheroes wear."

"Was there a Dr. Maniac display?" he asked.

I blinked. "Dr. Maniac? Why did you ask that?"

Mickey shrugged. "I think he's cool."

I stared at Mickey. I never thought he was into comics or superheroes before. Why did he mention that evil supervillain? Did he know something about me?

Or was I just being paranoid?

Walter let out another long burp, so loud it made his mask rattle. That was the signal for us to shut up so he could tell us about the video he wanted to make.

His three bulging eyes rolled around on his green face as he started to talk.

"The video is called *Mutant in the Basement*. We're all going to go down to the rec room and spread out the sleeping bags. George is going to record everything. Mason, Alonso, and Mickey will climb into their sleeping bags and pretend to be asleep. When I enter the room, you sit up and scream your heads off. Simple."

"You mean we're terrified of a kid wearing a mask?" Alonso said.

Mickey and I laughed.

Walter didn't. "Not funny. You're terrified of the mutant in the basement. It's basic, Alonso. Basic horror. Check your attitude, dude."

I moved closer to Alonso. "Don't start up with him," I whispered. "Let's just get this over with so we can have fun."

"Then what happens?" I asked. "After we scream."

"I know," Mickey said. "We grab the mutant. We wrestle him down to the floor. And we tickle him to death because mutants can't survive if they're tickled."

George laughed. He dove at Mickey, grabbed him from behind, reached around, and started tickling his belly with both hands. "Die, mutant, DIE!" he screamed.

Laughing, Mickey squirmed free. "Did you know there are these guys who tickle each other? It's like a sport. There are tickling teams. And they see who can take it the longest."

"That's stupid," I said.

"No. It's a thing," Mickey insisted. "I saw it on Netflix."

"No tickling," George said. "The mutant is going to rip all three of you to pieces. I have a special-effects app on my phone. The whole thing is going to be awesome CGI."

Walter let out a groan. "This mask is *smothering* me. And my face is going to itch off. Can we do this video now?"

So . . . that's what we did. We trooped down to the basement and prepared for the video scene.

Did it go the way George and Walter wanted?

Three guesses.

18

The rec room is huge. There are couches and chairs and a big game table. Air hockey and foosball. It's all warm and comfortable, with a thick shag rug over the floor.

Soft, pale moonlight washed into the room from a long window at the ceiling. The window was at ground level outside. Gazing up, I could see a little of the black sky through it.

Mickey, Alonso, and I spread out our sleeping bags and climbed inside. George dimmed the basement lights. He raised his phone and poked at the screen, getting the settings right.

Walter the Mutant waited behind the stairwell. He adjusted his mask. "Are you ready, George? I'm going to drown in sweat."

"Almost ready," George said, still working at his phone.

"Don't wake me. I'm going to sleep for real," Mickey said. He was tucked in up to his chin.

"Ready," George finally announced. He raised his phone. "Okay. I'm going to count off, 'One . . . two . . . three . . . Action.' You guys start sleeping. And don't laugh or anything. Make it look real."

"I'm going to walk in from here," Walter said from the stairway. "I'm going to come in slow, like a mutant checking out his prey. George will give you a signal when it's time for you to sit up and scream."

So Mickey, Alonso, and I shut our eyes and settled back in our sleeping bags. George counted down to *Action*. I heard Walter begin to shuffle into the scene.

And suddenly I heard a long, low buzz coming from one of the backpacks.

The Night Howler signal!

My heart skipped a beat. I sat straight up.

"Cut! CUT!" George screamed. He lowered his phone. "Mason—you ruined it. It looked awesome and you ruined it. You sat up too soon."

"S-sorry," I stammered. "I thought you gave the signal."

Mickey and Alonso shook their heads and laughed. "Smooth move, Mason," Alonso said.

I heard the buzz again from my phone.

"Okay. Take two," George said. "This time, wait for my signal, Mason."

"I . . . can't," I said. My heart was pounding. "I have to go." I scrambled out of my sleeping bag.

Cries of surprise all around.

"You can't go. We need to finish the scene," Walter said.

"What's your problem? You feel sick?" George demanded.

"Uh . . . yeah. Sick," I said. "Sorry, guys."

I stepped over Alonso in his sleeping bag and crossed to the pile of backpacks on the floor. I shoved a couple of them out of the way and grabbed mine.

I had to get away from them and climb into my costume. I had to find out where my mission was.

"No need to call my parents," I said. "I'm just going to walk home. Maybe the fresh air—"

Mickey burst up beside me. "That's *my* backpack, Mason. You got the wrong one."

"No," I insisted. "You're wrong."

He swiped the backpack out of my hands. "I'll show you."

"No—! Give it back!" I cried.

The zipper made a loud buzz as Mickey tugged it open all the way. He tilted the backpack upside down. And everything came tumbling to the floor.

"Oops. My bad," Mickey said. "It *is* yours."

I gasped. My costume spread out at my feet. I bent to grab it up. But Mickey was already staring at it.

"What's that?" he cried. He lifted the costume top with the NH insignia on the front and held it up for everyone to see. "Check this out!"

Too late to grab it and try to hide it.

My breath caught in my throat.

George hurried over to us. "I recognize that," he said. "That's the costume the Night Howler wears."

I'm dead meat.

I'm done.

It's over.

19

"Whoa. Mason, did you get that at the comic art museum?" Alonso asked.

I nodded. "Yes. That's where I got it."

Now I really *did* feel sick.

George raised the tights in front of him. "Is it spandex or what?"

"I guess." I sighed. "I don't know."

"We can use it in the video," Walter said. He tugged off the monster mask. His face was bright red and dripping with sweat. "Totally cool. The Night Howler can battle the mutant."

I didn't reply. I seriously felt like bursting into tears.

Cory, the old Night Howler, had trusted me. He trusted me with the secret of the Night Howler. And the powers that came with the costume.

I had let him down.

I'd let the world down.

And now the useless costume was going to be used in a dumb YouTube video.

I had to bite my lip really hard to keep from sobbing.

But then I had an idea.

"It's only pajamas," I said. "Not a real costume."

Mickey spread the dark cape out between his hands. "Pajamas don't have capes," he said.

"It's a bonus thing," I said. "You get the cape when you buy the pajamas."

George handed the tights to me. "Yeah. Feels like pajamas," he said. "Why'd you buy it?"

"Uh . . . I didn't," I said. "It was kind of a gift."

Not a lie.

"Quick. Put it on," Walter said. "This will be awesome. The mutant creeps into the basement. He plans to devour Alonso and Mickey in their sleeping bags. But the Night Howler arrives to rescue them."

"Cool," George said. "We'll work up some kind of battle between the two of you. I can add the SFX and sound effects later."

Alonso reached down and lifted the mask off the floor. "The pajamas come with a mask? Weird."

"Never mind," Walter said. "Put it on, Mason. Let's do it!"

I had no choice. I had to put the costume on.

But as I scrambled into it, my brain whirred with questions.

Will the costume still hold its powers?

Did I really fool them? Do they all believe it's just pajamas?

How do I get out of here? I have to find where my mission is.

I adjusted the cape around my shoulders and pulled the mask into place.

"Looking good, dude," Alonso said, stepping back to admire the costume. "It looks so real, Mason. Not like nerdy pajamas at all."

It feels real, too, I thought.

I could feel a gentle current rolling through the top.

So far, so good.

"You stand over there," George said. He pointed to a corner of the room. "Mickey and Alonso, sleep. The mutant walks in, ready to attack them. Then I'll give you a signal to come running into the scene."

I took a deep breath. I felt the power of the costume begin to surge.

"Why are you standing there?" George demanded. "Get moving, Mason."

"I don't think so," I said.

I raised my right arm. I moved my fingers in a slow rhythm.

And watched the dark cloud form over the basement ceiling.

YES!

I moved the cloud across the room and lowered it over my friends. They were lost in the deep shadow. I couldn't see them. Then I motioned with both hands, like a symphony conductor. I motioned slowly, letting the power of the costume do its thing.

Did I cloud their minds? If I did it correctly, they wouldn't remember a thing when the cloud lifted. They wouldn't even remember I was there.

I watched for a few seconds, hoping my shadow cloud would work. Then I spun away and ran full speed up the basement steps.

Feeling the power shoot through my body, I tore through the house and out the front door. Into a warm, starless night. The air was heavy and damp.

"Okay, I'm ready for action!" I said. I grabbed my phone and read the message on the screen.

20

Wreckage.

The evil criminal named Wreckage was in my neighborhood.

That's what the message on my screen told me.

Wreckage would be coming by any second. My job was to chase after him and capture him.

I had read about Wreckage. He recently broke up with his partner, Damage. But he was still a member of the dangerous criminal club known as the Wrecking Crew.

Wreckage and his pals didn't care about getting rich. They only liked to wreck things.

I tucked my phone into my costume as I heard the squeal of a car burst around the corner. That had to be him. Wreckage enjoyed wrecking all the cars he drove.

The car sped past me, tires skidding on the street as it picked up speed. I ducked my head, swept my cape behind me—and took off in the shadows. Running hard, carried by the dark mists, I caught up to the car.

With a burst of speed, I leaped onto the back of his car. I pulled myself over the trunk and spread myself out over the roof.

The car squealed around a corner.

I gasped, feeling myself slide off the side. Grappling with both hands, I kept myself from falling.

It was late. The streets of Fargo Hills were empty. The car swerved wildly from curb to curb. Wreckage was a *terrible* driver! Somehow I managed to climb to my knees. I balanced on the car roof, both hands out at my sides, like a tightrope walker.

The hot wind battered me this way, then that. But I kept my balance and rode through the dark streets. I knew where Wreckage was headed. Downtown.

But I didn't know why until he spun the car into a wide parking spot. I held on with both hands as the car made a hard stop and crashed into the car parked in front of it.

I jumped down, landed on my feet, and struggled to catch my breath. I shook my head hard, shaking away my dizziness.

The car door slammed. I turned to see Wreckage run toward a darkened store. I raised my eyes to see the sign at the top of the door.

MARK'S FINE JEWELRY.

I heard the shattering of glass. Wreckage smashed through the glass door of the store. A robbery!

I swept back my cape and took a deep breath. I felt the power of the costume pulsing through me.

I tossed back my head and gave the Night Howler howl.

"Aaaaaaaaawoooooooooooooh!"

I grabbed the door carefully, trying to avoid the shards of broken glass, and burst into the jewelry store.

A dim circle of light from the back of the store sent a faint glow over the rows of display cases. Wreckage bent over a glass case near the far wall, preparing to smash it with his fist—but he stopped when he saw me.

"Night Howler!" he cried. "I'm going to wreck this store. Then I'm going to wreck *you!*"

"You're not wrecking anyone tonight," I said. My voice sounded muffled in the small store. "This robbery isn't going to happen."

A thin smile spread slowly across his face. "Yes, it is."

I took a few steps toward him. I realized my heart was pounding. I trusted the power of my costume. But I was still new at this. I didn't know the best way to succeed. I was making it up as I went along.

I raised my hand high to summon a dark shadow. *I will trap him in the shadow cloud,* I thought, *and take him prisoner.*

But he had a surprise for me.

A bad surprise.

21

Wreckage grinned at me, his dark eyes flashing. "This robbery *is* going to happen, Night Howler. Because I am not alone!"

I heard a cough. Then the shuffle of feet on the floor.

An orange-costumed figure strode quickly out from the office at the back of the store. His face was covered in a tight orange mask that revealed only his eyes. His costume was tight, too, as if it had been painted on.

As he stepped forward, his hands moved quickly. At first, I thought he was carrying a small fire, a burst of flames. But as he moved closer, I saw clearly what he had between his hands.

Knives. Long-bladed knives. And the knives were on fire.

He was juggling flaming knives!

"Meet The Juggler!" Wreckage cried. "My talented new partner. He's going to entertain you while I wreck the store and help myself to these lovely jewels."

"No way—" I started.

But the Juggler stepped in front of me. The three knives flew in a circle around his moving hands. As he juggled them, he brought the flames closer and closer to my face.

I tried to step back. But I bumped into a display case.

The dazzling yellow flames were blinding me. I could hear Wreckage smashing display cases at the back of the store. But I couldn't see past the fiery knives floating in front of me.

Wreckage laughed. "The Juggler is an entertaining fellow, isn't he, Night Howler? Are you enjoying his act?"

"You won't get away with this," I said, blinking in the swirling bright yellow lights. I ducked my head as the flames swept over me.

"Of course we will," Wreckage said. I heard the clink of jewelry falling into his bag. "You have no power against the Juggler."

"Yes, I do," I said. I reached out both hands— and took the knives from the Juggler. He cried out as I tossed them in rhythm, the same rhythm he had used.

"Hey, wait—!" He couldn't hide his surprise.

I juggled the three flaming knives in front of his chest. He stumbled back. I kept the knives flying and forced him toward the back of the store.

Wreckage looked up from the jewelry case, his eyes wide with surprise. "You juggle?"

"I went to Circus Camp," I said. "I've been juggling since I was six."

I tossed the knives to the floor and stomped on them to put out the flames. "You're both dead meat," I said.

I raised my right hand and started to summon a dark cloud to trap them. But that's when I heard running footsteps behind me. Startled, I gasped and spun around.

And saw a blur of red race into the store. A woman in a bright red costume. Blinking, I stared at her red mask. And then I saw a blue insignia on the front of her costume.

I recognized her. Blue Strawberry!

The Juggler turned and scowled at her. "What kept you so long? He almost got us!"

22

"Don't move, Strawberry!" I cried. "These jewel thieves are my prisoners."

"You're a peach, Night Howler," she replied. "You're so sweet. You don't know when you've been sliced."

I knew I had to create a shadow cloud to hold all three of them. But was I too late?

"You're such a good guy," Blue Strawberry said, her eyes flashing from behind her red mask. "I'm going to give you some dessert."

She raised both hands above her head. "Enjoy!"

I felt something hit my shoulder. Something bounced off the top of my head.

"Huh?" I raised my eyes and saw—fruit. Fruit falling from the ceiling.

An apple. Then a bunch of bananas. A hard plum.

I ducked and tried to cover my head. A storm of grapes rained down on me. So heavy and thick I couldn't see.

I tried to squirm out from under the barrage of fruit. But it all came down too fast and too hard.

Oranges bounced in front of me. A melon crashed onto my shoulder and sent me collapsing to the floor.

It sounded like thunder. A rainstorm of fruit piling up all around. And when it finally stopped— there was silence.

I climbed slowly to my feet. I shook off my dizziness and stared at a tall wall of fruit.

"Hey!" I shouted. "Hey—you can't do this!"

Of course, there was no reply.

I lowered my shoulder and smashed forward, sending the fruit tumbling to the floor. Breathing hard, I stared around the store.

Empty.

The three criminals had escaped.

I shook my head. And pictured Blue Strawberry in her red costume with the bright blue fruit on the front. And muttered, "Looks like the Night Howler has a new enemy."

SLAPPY HERE, EVERYONE.

Maybe Mason should give up the hero act and open a *fruit store*! Hahaha!

When it comes to being a superhero, he's definitely a *lemon*!

How is he ever going to defeat a strawberry? He's only a shortcake! Hahaha!

Of course, he hasn't faced Dr. Maniac yet.

I'm sure he'll easily defeat Dr. Maniac.

Not!

Hahahaha!

23

I hurried home and quickly tucked the Night Howler costume back under the loose floorboard. I tried to go to sleep. But every time I closed my eyes, I saw a storm of fruit raining down on me.

I was desperate to ask Cory, the old Night Howler, about Blue Strawberry. Did he know her, too? Did he have a way to defeat her tornado of fruit? Did he have *any advice at all* for me?

But Cory was gone. He left no way for me to contact him. No phone number. No way to send a message.

He wanted me to be on my own, I guessed. And that's the way I felt that night—totally on my own.

The next day was Sunday. I played basketball on the playground court with Alonso and Mickey. They told me about the sleepover at George and Walter's house.

"Why weren't you there?" Alonso asked me.

"Uh . . . I felt sick last night," I said. "Mom said I couldn't go."

They didn't remember a thing. At least I did that right.

I should have felt great about having the awesome power to make people forget. But I couldn't stop thinking about Wreckage and the Juggler, and what a horrible failure I was.

Later at home, I had the strong feeling that Stella was watching me. Watching me more intensely than usual.

Did she suspect something? Or was I just being paranoid again?

I went upstairs to do a little homework. The door to my room was open. Had I left it open? I usually close it to keep Stella out.

Of course, I couldn't concentrate on my homework. I kept thinking about how my life had suddenly changed.

I loved being a superhero. I'd had fantasies about being a superhero my whole life. When I was a tiny kid, I put a towel around my neck and pretended it was a cape. I threw myself down the stairs. I thought I was Superman. I thought I could fly.

It was a painful lesson. But it didn't stop me from dreaming.

Yes, being a superhero was my dream job. And I didn't want it to end. I didn't want Stella finding out my secret and spoiling everything. Not Stella or anyone else.

And I wanted a chance to be successful. I wanted a chance to triumph over evil.

Wouldn't you know it? My chance came that night.

My phone buzzed. I reached for it and read the secret message:

You have an appointment with Dr. Maniac tonight.

The doctor is making a house call. Robbing a house on Forrest Hills Road.

My hands shook as I held the phone close and stared at the words.

My biggest challenge had come so soon.

Was I ready for it?

24

I heard my parents walking around downstairs. I knew I couldn't wait for them to go to sleep. I had to get to the house on Forrest Hills Road as fast as I could. I had to catch Dr. Maniac in the act.

So I pulled my Night Howler costume from its hiding place. My hands were trembling as I put it on. Not trembling from fright—trembling from excitement.

The old Night Howler quit the superhero business because he couldn't capture Dr. Maniac. The supervillain was the biggest challenge a superhero could face. And I was desperate to prove that I was up to the challenge.

I pulled the dark mask over my face. Then I swept the cape over my shoulders. I raised my hand and moved my fingers. And watched as a dark shadow floated over me.

Keeping in the shadow cloud, I made my way downstairs. Mom and Dad were sitting across from each another in the living room. They were tapping away on their tablets. They like to play Scrabble on their iPads. Mom always wins. Dad says it's just because he always picks bad letters.

I walked right between them. They didn't even notice the shadow as it floated past them.

Out the front door. I closed it silently behind me. And stepped into a warm, damp night. Low clouds covered the moon. Warm raindrops hung in the air.

Our neighbors were having a party in the house across the street. Cars filled the driveway and lined the curb. All the lights were on, and hip-hop pounded from the front windows.

I used both hands to raise the shadow cloud higher—and felt my shoes lift off the ground. Flying! I was flying. What an awesome feeling! Like living a dream.

I made myself float higher. The air rushed at me, hot and wet. I flew over a group of teenagers rolling down the middle of the street on skateboards. I felt like shouting down at them, giving them a good scare.

But I held myself back. *Save it for Dr. Maniac,* I told myself.

And as I floated across town, peering down at cars and houses, I suddenly began to grow more serious. I mean, I started to lose confidence. Maybe reality was setting in.

What makes me think I can go up against a foe like that supervillain?

Am I forgetting that I'm just a kid?

The old Night Howler tried and failed.

What makes me think I won't fail, too?

"I'm DOOMED!" The words burst from my throat.

And suddenly, there was the house below me. So lost in my dark thoughts, I hadn't even realized I had reached Forrest Hills Road.

The house was enormous, surrounded on all four sides by tall pine trees. The black roof tilted sharply. Three chimneys poked up like dark towers. The garage was a separate building in back. It was wide enough to hold at least four cars.

I lowered myself slowly to the ground in the big backyard. The pine trees shivered all around me in a strong breeze. I landed in tall grass that hadn't been mowed in a long time.

I gazed at the house. Only a few windows were lit. I turned and checked out the garage. The doors were open. The garage was empty. That probably meant no one was home.

No one but Dr. Maniac.

He must have waited till everyone had left. That would give him all the time he needed to break into the house and rob it.

I crept through the tall grass. I ducked low beneath a kitchen window and listened.

Silence.

I know you're in there, Maniac, I thought.

I raised myself high enough to peer into the window. No one in the kitchen. Dishes stacked on the counter and at the sink. One ceiling light washing yellow light down over the room.

My throat suddenly felt tight. I bit down to stop my teeth from chattering. The Maniac was so close, just on the other side of this brick wall.

So close. I was standing so close to one of the most horrible villains in history.

Mason, what's your plan?

Surprise, I decided.

Dr. Maniac was definitely not expecting me. I had to use surprise to capture him. I had to be fast. Burst into the room. Throw a shadow over him. Capture him before he had a chance to turn around—before he even *saw* me.

I swept my cape behind me. I felt a shudder of fear roll down my back. My teeth began to chatter again. No way to stop them.

I took a deep breath and grabbed the back doorknob. I expected the door to be locked. But to my surprise, it slid open easily.

I took another deep breath and stepped into the kitchen. It was warm inside and smelled of something sweet, like a cake that had been recently baked.

I ignored my pounding heart and my trembling legs. I crept through the kitchen to an open doorway. I gritted my teeth. Adjusted my mask. Let the power of the costume pulse through me.

Then I lowered my head and took off, running to the next room.

I had gone only a few steps when I heard several voices shout out: "HAPPY BIRTHDAY!"

25

I stopped short—and tripped over my cape. I stumbled across the dining room and ran into the windowsill. Quickly, I spun around and stared at the family around the table.

A father and mother and three kids huddled over a tall blue-and-white birthday cake at the end of the table. A little boy was on his knees on a chair, about to blow out the flickering candles.

The father's eyes went wide as I lurched toward them, and he opened his mouth in a scream. The birthday boy nearly fell off the chair. But the mother caught him in time. His two sisters moved behind the table, unable to hide their shock.

The mother laughed. "Gary, did you hire a superhero for Shawn's birthday? What a great surprise."

"Huh?" Gary shook his head. "Myra, I didn't hire him. Did *you* hire him?"

"Who is he supposed to be? Batman?" the birthday boy asked.

"I'm the Night Howler," I said, finally finding my voice. "I'm sorry, but—"

"You're the one who always howls?" Myra, the mother, said.

"Well, yes," I said. "But you see—"

"Did you bring balloons?" one of the girls asked.

"Yes. Aren't you supposed to bring balloons when you do a birthday party?" the father asked.

"I'm not *doing* your birthday party!" I shouted. "I'm in the *wrong house*!"

That got them quiet.

"I'm really sorry," I said, lowering my voice. "I made a big mistake. I shouldn't be here." I started toward the kitchen. "Pretend this didn't happen, okay? I'm totally embarrassed."

"Can you howl for us?" the birthday boy asked.

"I don't think so," I said. "But happy birthday anyway."

Holding my cape in both hands, I swept out of the room, through the kitchen, and out the back door. My face felt hot behind my mask. I knew I was still blushing from my mistake.

Oh, well. At least I gave them a birthday they won't forget, I told myself.

I ducked through an opening between the tall pine trees. The house next door came into view behind rows of low shrubs. The house was completely dark. No moonlight to reflect in the tall black windows.

I made my way to the stoop that ran along the front of the house. To my surprise, the door was wide open.

That was careless of Dr. Maniac, I thought. *Maybe he's slipping. Slacking off. Maybe he'll be easy prey.*

I took several deep breaths and prepared for battle. I crept up to the front steps, tossed back my head, and uttered the Night Howler howl:

"Aaaaaaaaawoooooooooooooh!"

I leaped onto the stoop.

And Dr. Maniac stepped out the front door. "You're late," he said.

26

I gasped and nearly toppled off the stoop.

"Huh? How d-did you know I was coming?" I stammered.

"I didn't," he said. "But you're late."

He stared down at his wrist, pretending he wore a watch. "You know, showing up on time is an important part of being a superhero."

I swallowed. I took a moment to gather my courage. "Well, I'm here now," I said, lowering my voice.

He squinted at me. "Are you sure? Can any of us be sure where we really are? Perhaps we are a figment of someone's imagination. Perhaps we are just characters in a novel, and we have no control over our actions."

"That's crazy," I said.

"I'm not crazy—I'm a MANIAC!" he screamed.

"Well, I'm the Night Howler," I said. "And I've caught you robbing this house."

"I know who you are," Dr. Maniac replied. "I

recognized the howl." He leaned close. "You know, if you want to sneak up on someone and take them by surprise, it's probably not a good idea to howl so loud."

"Thank you for the advice," I said. "But I repeat. I've caught you robbing this house."

"No, you haven't," he said. He brushed back his leopard-skin cape.

"Yes, I have."

"No, you haven't. You've caught me standing on the front stoop of this house."

I let out a long breath. Arguing with this dude was tough. I tried again. "I know you are here to rob this house."

"I don't rob houses," he replied. "I rob things *in* houses."

"I see you like word games," I said. "But the game is over. I'm bringing you to the police."

"No, you're not," he said, sticking out his chin.

"Yes, I am." I raised my hand to summon a shadow to trap him in.

Suddenly, he raised his eyes and turned his gaze to the street. His mouth dropped open in shock. "Oh, good heavens!" he cried. "Look at THAT!"

Startled, I spun around. I didn't see anything in the street. Total darkness.

"Made you look!" Dr. Maniac said. He tossed back his head and laughed. Then he disappeared into the house.

I let out another sigh. This guy was going to be a challenge.

I followed him into the house. A lamp in the entryway sent a yellow glow over the front rooms. My eyes adjusted slowly to the pale light. I saw a large living room filled with heavy-looking wooden furniture. To the left, a dining room with an endless table surrounded by tall chairs.

I heard Maniac clumping around in the living room. I stepped in and clicked on a ceiling light. He was hunched over a wide desk against the wall. He pulled open drawers and tossed things into the leopard-skin bag he was holding.

"Howler, help me move this desk," he called.

My mouth dropped open. "You want me to *help* you?"

"There is a hidden safe filled with jewelry under the floor," he said. "If you help me move the desk out of the way, I'll give you something shiny as a souvenir."

"No way! You're crazy!" I cried.

"I'm not crazy!" he screamed. "I'm a MANIAC!"

He jumped onto the desk and did a wild tap dance. His feathery boots thudded loudly against the hard wood desktop.

After a minute or so, he leaped back down to the floor. "It's important to express your feelings," he said. "Don't let them all get bottled up inside you."

He took a few steps toward me. For the first time, I noticed he had one brown eye and one blue eye. "Howler, come on." He motioned with both gloved hands. "You want to dance with me?"

I stumbled back. "No way!"

"It's good to go with the flow," he said. "Easy-breezy. I mean, sometimes I feel like a giraffe in a luggage store. Do you know what I mean?"

"No," I said. "I don't understand you at all."

"Howler, open your heart," he said, suddenly gushing with emotion. "Open your heart to your true feelings!" Teardrops rolled down his face.

That's enough, I decided.

"Oh, shut up!" I cried. "Shut up! You're not getting away, Maniac. So stop all the talk!"

"I'm only human," he said softly, as if I had hurt his feelings. "I'm like everyone else. I like to stand on a hilltop and spit at the clouds."

"Shut up! Shut up!" My head was spinning. I knew what he was trying to do. But I wasn't going to fall for all his double-talk.

I raised my right hand above my head. I gestured with my fingers. I could feel the pulsing current run from the costume and up my arm.

A dark shadow formed above me from out of nowhere. I moved my arm forward and sent the shadow floating low over Dr. Maniac.

"Your night is over," I told him. "You've been captured by the Night Howler. And I'll be howling in victory when you go to prison."

His grin didn't fade. "No, you won't," he said.

"Yes, I will."

"No, you won't," he repeated. "Look behind you, Howler."

"Ha," I said. "I'm not falling for that a second time."

"You should listen to him," a voice said from behind me. "You should turn around."

"Huh?" I gasped in shock and spun to the doorway. "Oh no!" I cried. "YOU again?"

27

Blue Strawberry strode into the room. Her red costume looked like a streak of fire under the bright ceiling light. Her eyes flashed behind the red mask.

"What's the matter, Night Howler?" she cried. "Orange you glad to see me?"

"Whoa. I'll handle the jokes!" Dr. Maniac protested.

"Just handle the jewelry," she replied. She motioned to me. "Why do I have to keep rescuing everyone from this pest?"

"Because he's a pest?" Maniac said.

Blue Strawberry helped Dr. Maniac shove the desk aside. Then he pulled up a secret trapdoor and opened a safe hidden there.

"Leave the jewels where they are," I ordered them. "You're not taking them."

"Yes, we are," Maniac said. He pulled up a diamond necklace and dropped it into his bag.

"No, you're not," I said. "I have enough power to imprison you both in shadow."

"No, you don't," Blue Strawberry said.

A loud *clink clink* echoed across the room as Dr. Maniac tossed more jewelry into his bag.

Blue Strawberry squinted at me through her mask. "You look like you need a snack. Today is Sunday, right? How about a nice Pineapple Sunday?" She waved both arms above her head.

"OWW!" I uttered a cry as something heavy and hard dropped from the ceiling, landed on my head, and bounced to the floor. Pain shot down my body. "Owww!" I couldn't dodge away. Another object hit my shoulder, nearly knocking me down.

Pineapples!

A storm of pineapples, heavy as bowling balls, sharp and prickly, rained down on me. I tried to shield myself but they dropped too fast. The pain sent me to my knees.

A pineapple smashed the top of my head. Red and bright whites flashed in front of me. I couldn't see. I hit the floor. Then everything went black.

How long did I lie there? I have no idea.

I finally raised my head. My whole body ached and throbbed from the pineapple attack. Groaning, I pulled myself to my knees and gazed around.

Of course, they were both gone.

Another major fail by the Night Howler.

But I had learned something important. I had to defeat Blue Strawberry before I would ever score a victory over another villain.

But . . . how?

28

Two nights later, I had a major supervillain in my control.

OverTime. He was known everywhere as one of the fastest, greediest, nastiest villains of all time. He was called OverTime because he worked all hours to commit crimes. His motto was "I'm never off duty. I work overtime!"

And now I had him cornered in the back of a supermarket he was robbing. I gave my Night Howler howl: *"Aaaaaaaaawooooooooooooooh!"* And I raised my arms to cover him in shadow.

He spun around in surprise. His black cape swirled behind him. He had a big white O on the front of his black shirt. And his big silver belt buckle was also shaped like an O.

"I'm too fast for you, Night Howler," he cried. "I'm actually robbing two stores at once. I'm robbing the vitamin store next door at the same time I'm talking to you."

"But—" I started.

"I work overtime," he said. "You have to work overtime to catch me." He turned and started to pull stacks of cash from the cash register.

"But I *have* caught you," I said. "Put down the bag. I'm taking you to the police." I raised my arms again, preparing to cast a shadow over him.

"But I'm not here. I'm next door," he replied. "You have to be two places at once to bring me in." He dumped more money into his bag.

"Okay, okay," I said. "I've captured *half* of you. I'll bring you in, and your other half will follow."

He tossed back his head and laughed. "You're too late, Howler. I'm already across the street. I'm getting away while you stand there. You have to work overtime to catch OverTime."

I scratched my head. Was he trying to pull a fast one? Or was he telling the truth?

I could see him clearly. He was moving fast, running from cash register to cash register, emptying them as fast as he could. Was it possible that he was across the street at the same time, escaping from me?

I waved my hands above my head. A dark cloud formed above me. I motioned it forward. Then I lowered it slowly over OverTime. He stopped moving as the shadow slid down over his head, his shoulders, his body. The loot bag fell from his hand.

"Let me out of here!" he shouted. "Let me out!"

I had him.

My heart was beating hard under my costume. Finally—a victory! I felt like celebrating.

My victory lasted about ten seconds.

Then I heard the familiar female voice behind me: "Hey, Howler, have you tried the cantaloupes?"

"*YAAAII!*" I cried out as a heavy melon dropped from the ceiling and crashed to the floor inches in front of me.

"Blue Strawberry!" I uttered. I spun around to face her.

I tried to dodge away, but I wasn't fast enough. Another cantaloupe dropped from above. Pain shot down my body as it bounced off my shoulder.

"Okay, okay. I know when I'm beat!" I said. I raised my hands above my head in surrender. "Take him. Take him, Blue Strawberry. You win again."

"I'm already gone," OverTime said. "You have to work overtime to catch me!"

I ducked as another heavy melon came crashing down. It splattered on the floor and sent a wave of goo over my boots.

When I looked up, they were both gone.

I let out a long sigh. I shook my head sadly.

Another horrible defeat.

As a superhero, I was a total failure. And it was all Blue Strawberry's fault.

Why was she determined to ruin my superhero career? Who was she?

I found out.

29

After dismissal the next day, my friends George and Walter were on the soccer field behind the school, working on a new horror video. I recognized Mickey and Alonso, even though they were wearing ugly orange masks covered in black warty spots and dangling eyeballs.

"How do we look?" Alonso asked as I trotted over to them.

I pretended to study him. "Did you get a haircut?"

"Ha," he replied. "You're a riot, Mason."

George had his phone raised. He motioned me away with his other hand. "Move it, Mason," he said. "We're shooting a scene."

"What's this video called?" I asked. "*Weirdos on the Playground?*"

"You are seriously not funny," Walter said. "The new video is going to be awesome. It's called *Martians from Montana.*"

"Huh?" My mouth dropped open. "How can Martians be from Montana?"

Walter grinned. "See? Got you thinking already! It's not your typical horror video, Mason. It makes you think. It makes you question things."

"You wouldn't understand it," his twin said.

"This mask is hot," Mickey complained, lifting it off. "Look. My face is sweating."

"Put it back," George told him. "We can shoot the scene—if Mason would just back off."

I took a couple of steps away. "Okay, okay."

Across the field, some kids from the elementary school had started a soccer game. Their shouts rang out over the grass.

George groaned and lowered his phone. "Go tell them to shut up," he told Walter.

"*You* do it," Walter snapped. "Why do I have to do it?"

"We're going to hear them on the video," George said. "Go tell them to be quiet."

"Why me?"

"I'm the director today," George replied. "That means I'm the boss."

"Give me the phone," Walter said. He swiped at it. Missed. "I'll be the director. You go stop their game."

"I'm the director," George insisted. "You were the director of *Freakazoids from the Planet Freak*, remember? And it was seriously boring."

113

Walter stuck his chin out. "Was not."

"Yes, it was."

"Hey, guys—" Mickey said, pulling off his mask again.

Walter gave George a hard shove. The phone nearly slipped from George's hand.

George shoved the phone into his pocket. He punched his brother in the stomach.

Walter let out an *oooof* sound. He doubled over for a second. Then he charged at George and tackled him to the grass.

"Hey, guys—?" Mickey repeated.

I couldn't believe it. The twins were rolling in the grass, wrestling hard, grunting and groaning.

Are twins always like this?

Alonso had his phone raised and was recording the fight.

That's when I decided to step in.

I dropped down beside them. Grabbed Walter by the shoulders and struggled to tug him off George.

"Get off me!" he screamed. "Get off, Mason! I'll pound you! You're hamburger meat! I mean it!"

I tightened my grip and swung him off his brother. "Hamburger meat?"

George scrambled to his feet, gasping for breath.

I held on to Walter until he started to calm down. Then I let go and climbed to my feet. I had grass stains on my shirt and jeans. Sweat poured down my face.

My first victory, I thought. *Score one for the Night Howler!*

Forget Dr. Maniac and the supervillains. Maybe I should just break up playground fights from now on.

The two brothers bumped knuckles. George wiped dirt off his chin with the back of his hand.

Alonso waved his phone in the air. "I got it all on video," he declared. "Maybe we can work a fight scene into the story somewhere."

"Awesome," Mickey said through his mask. "These two brothers are so freaked by the Martians from Montana, they go berserk on each other."

"I didn't go berserk," Walter said. "George did."

"Did not," George snapped. "You tackled me."

"You punched me. You went berserk, bro."

George raised a fist. "You want to see berserk? I'll show you berserk!"

Mickey tossed his mask to the ground. "I've got to get home," he said. He turned and stomped away.

Alonso shrugged. "He's right. It's getting late." He handed his mask to Walter. His face was bright red and drenched in sweat.

"Okay. Break time," George said. "Break time, everybody! Be back on the set tomorrow afternoon!"

I think I'm the only one who heard him. Everyone had scattered by that time, even his brother.

I waved. "See you tomorrow," I said.

A heavy feeling washed over me as I walked home. I knew I wouldn't be the Night Howler for long if I kept blowing every mission. So far, I'd had fail after fail.

I gritted my teeth and fought back my disappointment. I *had* to have a victory. I *had* to defeat the next villain I faced. I promised myself I'd find a way to win.

At home, I climbed the stairs to my room and tossed my backpack onto the bed. Stella's door was open. "Hey, Stella—are you home?" I shouted.

No answer.

I pulled out my science notebook and carried it to my desk. I started to sit down when I saw something at my dresser. I squinted across the room.

"Something is wrong here," I murmured out loud. "Something is very wrong."

30

The bottom dresser drawer. It was open an inch or two.

I didn't remember opening it this morning.

I stared at it. Today was Wednesday. Not laundry day. So Mom or Dad would not have opened it.

I stepped away from the desk and glanced around my room. *Whoa. Wait.*

My closet door. I remembered clearly that I had left it open. I was late for school. In a hurry. I didn't close the door—but it was closed now.

My muscles tensed. My senses went on high alert.

What was that balled-up pair of socks doing on the floor beside my wastebasket? Had I tossed them there? No. I didn't think so.

I knew what had happened. I knew someone had been in my room.

And, of course, I knew who that someone was.

"Stella?" I shouted her name again. I stepped out into the hall. "Stella? Are you home?"

117

No answer.

She must be at her after-school guitar lesson.

I realized my hands were clenched into tight fists. I slowly unclenched them. I told myself to calm down.

Okay. Stella was snooping around in my room.

What was she looking for? Was she just snooping as usual for no reason?

I glanced at the loose floorboard where my costume was hidden. As far as I could tell, the floorboard hadn't been touched.

I folded my arms in front of my chest. Sometimes that helped me calm down. Then I crossed the hall into Stella's room.

I clicked on the ceiling light. Stella kept her room perfectly neat at all times. Everything in its place. Her walls were covered with photos and posters of her favorite singers and groups. They were all tacked up straight in neat rows.

Stella makes her bed every morning. How weird is that?

And she doesn't toss her dirty clothes on the floor like I do. She drops them all in the laundry hamper in the bathroom. Just to make me look bad, I think.

Her laptop was shut. Her desk wasn't littered with papers and books. Even her stuffed leopard that she used to sleep with stood up straight and alert on the top of her bookshelf.

What a freak!

I glanced all around. Why was I in her room? I wasn't sure. Was I just paying her back for snooping around in *my* room?

I turned and started to leave. But I stopped a few feet from the door.

Her closet was open a tiny bit. Without thinking, I started to cross the room.

The door squeaked as I pulled it open wider. Dresses and tops were all neatly hung up. I clicked on the closet light. On the floor, Stella's shoes were perfectly lined up.

Some old board games were stacked against the back wall. A basketball rested in the corner. *My* basketball. "So that's where the little thief hid it," I murmured.

And then something caught my eye at the far end of the closet. Something red, half-hidden behind some faded jeans, rolled up on the floor.

I ducked low and moved deeper into the closet. I stepped to the back and bent to lift up the red item. Clothing. Folded up into a ball.

Carrying it in my arms, I backed out of the closet. Then I unrolled it under the ceiling light. "Oh, wow!" I murmured.

I stared in shock at the red cape. I let the cape fall to the floor. I unrolled the red tights. And then the long-sleeved top with the blue insignia on the front.

119

My whole body started to shake. I knew what I was holding.

Blue Strawberry's costume.

"Stella!" Her name burst from my lips. "Stella!"

Stella was Blue Strawberry!

SLAPPY HERE, EVERYONE . . .

Hahaha. You know what I always say? Family comes first!

What's more important than family, everyone?

And if you're going to have a battle of super-heroes, why not keep it in the family?

Know what I would do if I were Mason?

I'd tear a biiiiiiig hole in Blue Strawberry's costume.

She'd never leave the house in it again! Hahaha.

See? That's why I'm a superhero. You think I'm just a beauty. But I have brains, too! Hahaha!

31

My hands trembled as I carefully rolled the costume back into a tight ball. My brain was doing flip-flops. I stepped back into the closet and stuffed the costume where I'd found it.

Then I hurried back to my room. I closed the door and threw myself onto the bed. I covered my head with my hands and shut my eyes.

I felt dizzy. I tried to breathe normally, but my chest was heaving, and my breath came out in fast gulps.

How could this happen?

How could my sister be my archenemy?

I jumped up and started to pace back and forth. I had to think. I had to figure this out.

How did it happen? How?

I thought maybe I knew. Maybe it happened that day we visited the comic art museum. Maybe the same thing that happened to me happened to Stella.

Maybe she met a superhero who wanted to

give it up. Like the Night Howler. He didn't want the job anymore. He convinced me to take it.

Maybe she ran into Blue Strawberry. Maybe Blue Strawberry wanted to retire, too. My sister would *grab* the chance to take on the job. What a perfect way to show she was better than me!

She knew I was the comic book fan in the family. But now she would be even greater than a fan. She would be an actual supervillain!

I ignored my dizziness as I paced back and forth. She must be having so much fun defeating the Night Howler night after night. And she must be so happy that no one knows her secret.

Well, I knew it now. And I wasn't going to pretend that I didn't.

I had to stop her. If I couldn't, I would never be a success as a superhero.

A few hours later, the four of us sat around the dinner table. Dad brought home a bucket of chicken. But I could barely choke down a tiny wing.

I kept staring across the table at Stella. She was in a great mood, talking nonstop about a history quiz she had aced, and how she slaughtered some girl in a tennis match after school, and how awesome her guitar teacher is.

She laughed and grinned and joked and didn't stop yakking.

I knew why she was in such a good mood. And it made me angrier and angrier.

After dinner, I followed Stella up to her room. I closed her door behind me.

She sat down on the edge of her bed and picked up her tablet. She began swiping the screen with her finger. She pretended I wasn't standing there.

I cleared my throat. "I know what you're doing," I said.

She didn't look up. Just kept swiping.

"I know what you're doing," I repeated, speaking more slowly.

She finally glanced up. "Looking at my friends' Instagram photos?"

"No," I said. "You—"

"I know, I know," Stella said, groaning. "I should be doing my homework instead of looking at these. But what do *you* care?"

I gritted my teeth. "That's not what I'm talking about, Stella." My hands were balled into tight fists. I took a deep breath so I wouldn't explode.

She lowered the tablet to her lap. "What's your problem, Mason?" she asked. Total innocent face.

"I know you're Blue Strawberry," I blurted out.

Her eyes went wide. "WHAT?"

"Blue Strawberry," I said. "Stop acting dumb, Stella. I know your secret."

She blinked a few times. Then she squinted hard at me as if studying me. "My secret? I don't get the joke, Mason."

She was doing a great acting job. But I knew she was just stalling for time. I saw the costume in the closet. There was no way she could wriggle out of this one.

"Give up," I said. "I know you're Blue Strawberry."

She laughed. "If I'm Blue Strawberry, you're the Purple Cucumber."

I stared at her, clenching and unclenching my fists. I felt ready to explode again.

"You've been reading too many comic books," she said.

I spun around and started to cross the room to her closet. My plan was to pull out the Blue Strawberry costume and throw it in her face.

But halfway there, I heard my phone buzz in my room across the hall. The special Night Howler signal. I was being called on another mission.

"Gotta go," I said. I turned and darted to my room. I left her sitting there, staring at me with that phony innocent look on her face.

I grabbed my phone and read the message on the screen. A villain named Randy Revenge was holding up a fishing goods store. Stealing thousands of dollars' worth of expensive rods and reels.

I closed my bedroom door and pulled the Night Howler costume from its hiding place.

This was going to be a big night. I already had it planned.

I would go after Randy Revenge and capture him in a shadow. Blue Strawberry would follow me. But this time I'd be ready for her.

Before she could rain down any more fruit on me, I would capture her, too. And I would rip the mask off her face. And show Stella that I could no longer be fooled. Her game was up.

That was my plan.

And it worked. Almost.

32

I crept out of the house and ran down the front lawn toward the street. Halfway there, I turned back. The light was on in Stella's room.

Was she getting ready to help Randy Revenge?

I'd read about Randy Revenge in some graphic novels. He was huge and powerful and angry. He had biceps the size of soccer balls. Seriously. He could punch his fist right *through* you!

Randy had a bad childhood. And now he wanted revenge against the whole world. He got his revenge wherever he could. And his amazing super-strength allowed him to overpower anyone who tried to grab him.

I didn't plan to grab him. I planned to trap him in a shadow cloud. And tonight, I'd get MY revenge—by defeating Blue Strawberry.

I summoned a shadow and rode it in darkness to the fishing goods store. I stopped across the street and read the sign above the door: BAIT YOUR HOOK.

The store was dark. But through the big front window, I could see someone moving around in there. Randy Revenge! I heard a hard *thud* and then a crash. Randy was so big, he was knocking over display cases!

I tossed back my head and uttered the Night Howler howl: *"Aaaaaaaaawoooooooooooooh!"*

Then I darted across the dark, empty street. Grabbed the door handle at the front of the store. Ripped the door open and burst inside.

In the dim light, I saw Randy in the middle of the store. His gray tights and his cape shimmered like silver. He wore a sleeveless black midriff shirt to show off his muscles.

His arms were filled with fishing rods. He dropped them when he saw me enter. They clattered to the floor all around him.

He spun to face me. "Night Howler!" he growled. He had a deep, gravelly voice. It sounded more like choking than talking. "What are you fishing for? I hope it's not *me*!" he boomed.

"I'm fishing for compliments!" I said, sweeping my cape behind me. "All the compliments I'm going to get when I bring you in."

He snickered and took a few steps toward me. "I like you, Night Howler," he said. "So I'm going to be kind. I'm not going to torture you. I'm going to finish you off with just one quick punch."

He took another step closer. He raised his right arm and flexed his enormous bicep. "This will only hurt for a second," he snarled. "Then nothing will ever hurt you again."

My heart leaped into my throat. My legs began to tremble. But I knew I had to stay calm. Stay focused. He was big and strong. But I had powers he couldn't dream of.

"You don't scare me," I said, forcing my voice to stay steady. "I'm the Night Howler. My shadow will hold you no matter how strong you are."

I raised both hands to summon a shadow.

He swung his fist. His punch landed like a stone hammer in the middle of my chest.

I heard a ringing sound just before the pain bolted through my whole body.

My legs collapsed.

I crumpled to the floor.

I couldn't breathe. I couldn't move. A heavy darkness swallowed me.

He killed me.

33

Well . . . actually, he didn't kill me. He knocked me totally unconscious.

Trust me. It was like being dead.

I didn't see stars or hear bells ringing or birds chirping. I sprawled there in a heap on the floor, lost in total blackness.

How long was I out?

I don't know. But when I finally opened my eyes, the first thing I noticed was that my chest really hurt. I'm talking throbbing pain that made every breath hurt.

The second thing I noticed was that Randy Revenge was gone.

I struggled to sit up and glanced around. The fishing rods were gone, too. All of them. The store was bare.

Why did he want fishing rods? Why was he taking revenge on this store?

I would never know the answers. I had been

defeated again. I wasn't the Night Howler. I was the Night Loser.

I sat on the floor, still dazed. Breathing slowly in and out. Waiting for the pain in my chest to fade.

The sound of the door opening made my heart jump. I turned to the front with a groan. Pain soared over my chest.

I saw a flash of red. Boots clicked across the floor.

Blue Strawberry strode into the aisle. She stopped when she saw me on the floor.

"You're too late," I said. My voice came out hoarse and strained.

She squinted at me through her red mask.

"You're too late," I repeated. "You can't rescue Randy Revenge because he rescued himself. He's gone."

She didn't speak. Just stared down at me. I could see she was thinking hard.

"I know it's you," I said to her. "I saw the costume in your closet."

She blinked. "What?"

I suddenly realized I had her off guard. Maybe the night wouldn't be a total defeat after all.

"I know it's you," I repeated. "Your game is over."

"I . . . don't understand," she stammered.

Before she could move, I raised my hands and formed a dark shadow cloud above my head. I waved my hands forward and the shadow slid over Blue Strawberry.

I lowered it over her till she was trapped inside it.

I jumped to my feet. My chest throbbed with pain, but I ignored it. "Your little joke is over, Stella!" I cried.

I dove forward. Reached into the shadow. Grabbed her mask with both hands. And ripped it off her face.

"Oh noooo!" I cried.

34

I let out a scream and stared at the face of a woman I'd never seen before.

Not Stella. Not my sister.

Her green eyes flashed angrily.

I lost my concentration and the shadow cloud drifted away.

Blue Strawberry yanked the mask from my hands. "What's your problem, Night Howler?" she snapped. "You're acting like a super-psycho."

"I—I—I—" I sputtered.

"Maybe you need a nice cool dessert," she said. She raised both hands over her head.

I felt something wet and soft hit my shoulders. Something splattered the top of my head. I looked up and saw little chunks of fruit—hundreds of them—raining down on me.

Pineapple. Apples. Grapes. Fruit cocktail! A downpour of fruit cocktail, pounding me, thundering like a powerful waterfall.

I dropped to my knees and covered my head as the fruit splashed and thudded and battered me. When it finally stopped, my costume was drenched and sticky. I pulled chunks of pineapple off my shoulders. I shook the cape hard, tossing out pieces of fruit.

Of course, Blue Strawberry was gone.

Another night. Another major fail.

What kind of superhero was I? Wreckage, the Juggler, OverTime, Randy Revenge, Blue Strawberry—they had all escaped. I was a joke, that's what I was.

I hurried home. I knew there was only one way to prove that I deserved to be the Night Howler. I had to capture Dr. Maniac.

But would I even get the chance?

I darted up to my room and hid my costume under the floorboards. I pulled on my pajamas, still thinking gloomy thoughts about my defeat.

I jumped when Stella came bursting into my room. "You weren't in your room. Where were you?" she demanded.

"I just went downstairs for a glass of water," I said.

She narrowed her eyes at me, studying me.

"I owe you an apology," I said. "I was in your room. I saw that Blue Strawberry costume, and I thought—"

"That's my Halloween costume," Stella said.

134

"Cool, huh? Mom and Dad bought it for me at the comic art museum."

"Yeah. Cool," I muttered. "See you in the morning."

It took hours to get to sleep. My chest still throbbed, and I couldn't stop thinking about what a loser I was. I kept picturing the insane grin on Dr. Maniac's face. And I kept imagining myself grabbing him, twirling him around, burying him in deep shadow, all the time howling the Night Howler howl.

Two nights later, I had the chance to make it all come true.

I was asleep when the special buzz on my phone woke me up. The message on the screen told me that the evil supervillain was robbing another house across town.

"This is it," I murmured to myself. I could feel the excitement wash over my whole body. I pulled up my costume. My hands trembled as I tugged it on. The mask felt snug and warm against my face.

I took a deep breath and pushed back my cape. I started to my bedroom door.

"This is it. This is it," I kept repeating to myself. "The night for the Night Howler to *shine*!"

I pulled open the door and took a step into the

hall. I stopped. I heard something. Footsteps. Someone walking around.

Stella's room was dark. I listened. More footsteps. Someone on the stairs. Was Mom or Dad still awake?

I held my breath. All my muscles tensed. I listened some more.

And gasped as Dr. Maniac stepped off the stairway. His head bobbed up and down as he strode toward me with long, rapid steps.

"No need to look for me, Howler," he said in a harsh whisper. "Here I am."

35

"Uh...uh..." I was too shocked to speak. I backed into my room.

I couldn't think straight. The walls spun all around me. I could feel the blood pulsing at my temples.

Dr. Maniac followed me.

"What are you doing here?" I blurted out. "How did you find me?"

"I have an Enemy Tracker," Maniac said. "Don't you have one? You should order one online."

I took a deep breath. "I guess I *am* your enemy," I murmured. "I mean, I'm going to capture you."

He shook his head. "That makes me as unhappy as a moose in a BarcaLounger."

I cleared my throat. My brain was starting to work again.

"This is it," I murmured. "This is it."

"I have bad news and good news for you,"

Maniac rasped. "The bad news is that you are doomed."

"What's the good news?" I asked.

"The good news is it's not going to rain tonight! Hahaha!"

"You're crazy!" I cried.

"I'm not crazy—I'm a MANIAC!" he screamed. He moved toward me.

I raised both hands above my head. I formed a dark gray cloud. I motioned my hands to send the cloud floating over him.

I quickly lowered it. Covered in shadow and—

A beam of white light broke through the darkness.

I uttered a startled cry. Squinting, I saw the flashlight in Maniac's hand. A blinding, bright halogen flashlight.

His light cut through my shadow. Shattered it. Destroyed it.

Then he raised the circle of light to my face.

I covered my eyes. Too late. The hot white light glowed on my eyelids. Pain shot down my face.

"What's wrong, Howler?" Maniac cried. "Don't you enjoy the spotlight?"

His laughter rang off the walls.

He's right. I'm doomed, I realized. *It's over.*

36

He kept the light on my face. I covered my eyes with my arm. I could still see the glare.

Suddenly, I heard Maniac let out a cry.

The light fell from my face.

Blinking hard, I opened my eyes—and saw Blue Strawberry wrestling with Dr. Maniac. He tried to swing away from her. But she grabbed his hand and stole the flashlight from him.

He swiped for it, but she tossed it out the open window.

Through his mask, he glared at her angrily. "Hey—what's your problem? Whose side are you on?" he boomed.

I realized this was my chance. I raised both hands and formed another deep shadow. I sent it swirling over Maniac.

He thrashed at it with both hands. Tried to squirm out of it.

"Got you!" I cried.

I didn't have time to celebrate. Trapped in the

shadow, he staggered across the room. "Howler," he said, "do you know my frequent-flier number? Oh, never mind!"

Then he lowered his shoulder. Burst out of my shadow cloud. And jumped out the window.

I watched him fly away.

Then I turned back to Blue Strawberry. I shook my head. "He got away," I murmured. "But you saved my life. Thank you."

"No big deal," she said. She pulled off her mask.

"Oh, wow!" I cried.

It was Stella. Not Blue Strawberry. Stella in her Halloween costume.

"Mason, you owe me *forever*!" she said.

Yes, I owed her forever. Stella saved my life. But she also ended my career as a superhero.

She knew my identity. She saw me in the costume. That meant the costume lost all its powers. It was useless. And I was back to being twelve-year-old Mason Brady.

Later, I rolled up the Night Howler costume and stuffed it into a shopping bag. I begged my parents to take me back to the comic art museum. And they finally said yes.

It was a sunny Saturday afternoon. The museum was crowded with comic and superhero fans from all over.

My plan was to find a museum worker to return the costume to. But they all seemed to be busy.

My parents went to the restaurant to get coffee. I wandered down a long hall, searching for someone with a museum badge.

I stepped into a dimly lit room in a corner of the hall. I stopped to look at the superhero posters. A video was playing on a screen near the back.

I turned and started to leave when I saw Dr. Maniac standing beside the video screen. He was pulling off his leopard-skin cape.

He turned when he saw me approach.

"Are you an actor?" I said. "Do you work for the museum playing the part of Dr. Maniac?"

He shook his head. "No. I'm the real deal, kiddo. I'm Dr. Maniac." He didn't recognize me. He didn't know that I was the Night Howler.

He tugged off his mask.

"What are you doing?" I asked.

"I've had enough," he said. "The whole Maniac thing is stressing me out."

He folded the mask and set it down beside the cape.

"Huh?" I gasped. "You're really giving it up?"

He nodded and swept back his blond hair. "It's hard being a maniac, kid. All that shouting gives me a sore throat. And I'm tired of the narrow escapes. Too scary. Bad for my blood pressure."

I stared at him. I didn't know what to say.

He pointed at me. "Hey, I have an idea. Would *you* like to be Dr. Maniac?"

My mind spun. "Well . . ."

How much fun would it be? I asked myself.
A LOT!

Maniac smiled as he handed the cape and mask over to me. "Here. Don't forget the feather boots," he said. He bent and started to pull them off his feet.

My heart was racing with excitement as I stuffed the costume into my backpack.

"Hey, enjoy!" Maniac said, slapping me on the shoulder. "And good luck, kid."

"I'm not a kid," I said. "I'm a MANIAC!"

EPILOGUE FROM SLAPPY

Hahaha! Those are big boots to fill, Mason. Hope you're not allergic to feathers!

I think Mason will make a great villain—don't you? He was such a loser as a hero. He *has* to be better as a bad guy.

At least we know he'll be healthy. Blue Strawberry will always be there to make sure he has plenty of fruit in his diet! Hahaha.

Well, that's the exciting adventure for this time.

Let's all catch our breath. Then I'll be back with another scary Goosebumps story.

Remember, this is *SlappyWorld*.

You only *scream* in it!

About the Author

R.L. Stine says he gets to scare people all over the world. So far, his books have sold more than 400 million copies, making him one of the most popular children's authors in history. The Goosebumps series has more than 150 titles and has inspired a TV series and two motion pictures. R.L. himself is a character in the movies! He has also written the teen series Fear Street, and the Mostly Ghostly and Nightmare Room series. He is currently writing a series of graphic novels entitled Just Beyond. R.L. Stine lives in New York City with his wife, Jane, an editor and publisher. You can learn more about him at rlstine.com.

Catch the MOST WANTED Goosebumps® villains UNDEAD OR ALIVE!

SPECIAL EDITIONS

📖 SCHOLASTIC

scholastic.com/goosebumps

GBMW42

REVENGE OF THE LIVING DUMMY
R.L. STINE

CREEP FROM THE DEEP
R.L. STINE

MONSTER BLOOD FOR BREAKFAST!
R.L. STINE

THE SCREAM OF THE HAUNTED MASK
R.L. STINE

DR. MANIAC VS. ROBBY SCHWARTZ
R.L. STINE

WHO'S YOUR MUMMY?
R.L. STINE

MY FRIENDS CALL ME MONSTER
R.L. STINE

SAY CHEESE - AND DIE SCREAMING!
R.L. STINE

WELCOME TO CAMP SLITHER
R.L. STINE

■ SCHOLASTIC

www.scholastic.com/goosebumps

GBHL19H2

THE SCARIEST PLACE ON EARTH!

THE ORIGINAL Goosebumps BOOKS
WITH AN ALL-NEW LOOK!

R.L. Stine's Biography

CONTINUE THE FRIGHT
AT THE GOOSEBUMPS SITE
scholastic.com/goosebumps

FANS OF GOOSEBUMPS CAN:

- **G** PLAY THE GHOULISH GAME:
  GOOSEBUMPS: SLAPPY'S DROP DEAD HOUSE

- **G** LEARN ABOUT NEW BOOKS AND TERRIFYING CLASSICS

- **G** TAKE A QUIZ AND LEARN WHICH TYPE OF MONSTER YOU ARE

- **G** LEARN ABOUT THE AUTHOR WHO STARTED IT ALL: R.L. STINE

◼ SCHOLASTIC

GBWEB2

THE  SERIES COMES TO LIFE IN A BRAND-NEW DIGITAL WORLD

MEET Slappy—and explore the Goosebumps Zone.
PLAY games, create an avatar, and chat with other fans.

Start your
adventure today!
Download the
OME BASE app
and scan this
mage to unlock
clusive rewards!

SCHOLASTIC.COM/HOMEBASE

GOOSEBUMPS

SLAPPYWORLD

THIS IS SLAPPY'S WORLD—
YOU ONLY SCREAM IN IT!

SLAPPY BIRTHDAY TO YOU
R.L. STINE

ATTACK OF THE JACK!
R.L. STINE

I AM SLAPPY'S EVIL TWIN
R.L. STINE

PLEASE DO NOT FEED THE WEIRDO
R.L. STINE

ESCAPE FROM SHUDDER MANSION
R.L. STINE

THE GHOST OF SLAPPY
R.L. STINE

IT'S ALIVE! IT'S ALIVE!
R.L. STINE

THE DUMMY MEETS THE MUMMY!
R.L. STINE

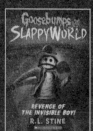

REVENGE OF THE INVISIBLE BOY!
R.L. STINE

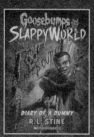

DIARY OF A DUMMY
R.L. STINE

THEY CALL ME THE NIGHT HOWLER!
R.L. STINE

MY FRIEND SLAPPY
R.L. STINE

31901065902936